Superman's Final Battle

Amid smoke and flames, Superman tackled the Doomsday monster and dragged him into the air where, he hoped, Doomsday could do no more harm. But Doomsday wasn't ready to give up. He raked Superman with his arm-spikes, ripping a gash in the Man of Steel's powerful chest.

Superman gasped in agony. Until now, he had been victorious in the battles he had fought. He had confronted Doomsday, almost certain of his eventual triumph. Now he wasn't sure he could stop the creature.

Then Doomsday raised his fist and smashed Superman with a shattering blow that hurled him unconscious to the ground.

Doomsday roared with victory.

Other books of related interest

STAR WARS®

TEENAGE MUTANT NINJA TURTLES®

THE YOUNG INDIANA JONES CHRONICLES™

SUPERMAN®

DOOMSDAY™ & BEYOND

LOUISE SIMONSON

Interior pencil art by
DAN JURGENS

Interior inks by
JOSÉ LUIS GARCÍA-LÓPEZ

Superman created by Jerry Siegel and Joe Shuster

Bantam Books
New York · Toronto · London · Sydney · Auckland

RL 4.0, 008–012

SUPERMAN: DOOMSDAY & BEYOND
A Skylark Book / September 1993

Skylark Books is a registered trademark of Bantam Books,
a division of Bantam Doubleday Dell Publishing Group, Inc.
Registered in U.S. Patent and Trademark Office and elsewhere.

Cover painting by Alex Ross.
Interior pencil art by Dan Jurgens.
Interior inks by José Luis García-López.

Superman created by Jerry Siegel and Joe Shuster.

ISBN 0-553-48168-1

Published simultaneously in the United States and Canada

*Bantam Books are published by Bantam Books, a division of Bantam
Doubleday Dell Publishing Group, Inc. Its trademark, consisting of
the words "Bantam Books" and the portrayal of a rooster, is Registered
in U.S. Patent and Trademark Office and in other countries. Marca
Registrada. Bantam Books, 1540 Broadway, New York, New York 10036.*

PRINTED IN THE UNITED STATES OF AMERICA

OPM 0 9 8 7 6 5 4 3 2 1

To my mother, Louise Jones, who took me
to the library every week,

and to my husband, Walter, who believes a
person can never have too many books.

Acknowledgments

With admiration and thanks to Jerry Siegel and Joe
Shuster, creators of Superman; to Jack Kirby, who
gave us a new visual vocabulary for super-heroes; to
Mike Carlin, Superman editor extraordinaire—without whom none of this would be possible; and to
Charles Kochman, for his unfailing good judgment
and good humor.

This book was primarily adapted from the story serialized in the following comic books, originally published by DC Comics:

Man of Steel #1-6 (limited series, 1986)
Superman #73-82 (1992–93)
Superman in Action Comics #683-692 (1992–93)
Superman: The Man of Steel #17-26 (1992–93)
Adventures of Superman #496-505 (1992–93)

These comic books were created by the following people:

Editors:	Mike Carlin	Inkers:	Brett Breeding
	Andrew Helfer		Dick Giordano
			Doug Hazlewood
Assistant			Dennis Janke
Editors:	Jennifer Frank		Denis Rodier
	Frank Pittarese		Trevor Scott
Writers:	John Byrne	Colorists:	Glenn Whitmore
	Dan Jurgens		Tom Ziuko
	Karl Kesel		
	Jerry Ordway	Letterers:	John Costanza
	Louise Simonson		Albert DeGuzman
	Roger Stern		Bill Oakley
Pencillers:	Jon Bogdanove		
	John Byrne		
	Tom Grummett		
	Jackson Guice		
	Dan Jurgens		

Superman

Clark Kent

Jor-El

Lois Lane

Jimmy Olsen

Perry White

Lex Luthor II

Supergirl

Charlie

Doomsday

The Man of Steel

The Last Son of Krypton

Lara

Martha (Ma) Kent

Jonathan (Pa) Kent

Bibbo

Professor Hamilton

Mitch

Director Westfield

Dubbilex

Guardian

Superboy

The Cyborg

Mongul

Prologue

A mineral-encrusted coffin lay deep within the
Earth. Inside the metal vault, an evil creature,
swathed from head to toe like a high-tech mummy,
struggled against the fraying cables that restrained
him. Finally, one of his bonds snapped. The being's
left arm was free. Beneath the earth, he laughed like
the crack of doom.

"Jonathan, look! A meteor!" Martha Kent watched
openmouthed as a ball of fire streaked through
the skies and slammed into a snow-covered wheat
field. The impact rattled the windows of their old
farmhouse.

"Whatever it was hit in the north forty," said
Jonathan Kent. "Come on!"

There, in the middle of a snowy field, they found
a hole, deep as a man is tall.

"Look in the center!" said Martha as they clambered into the hole. "Must be some kind of rocket."

Jonathan peered through a frosted window. "Looks like there's something alive inside. Maybe one of those animals scientists have been studying to see how they survive in space."

Suddenly Jonathan leapt back. "It's opening. There's something in there!"

"It's a baby!" cried Martha. She lifted the naked infant into her arms. "Someone put a little baby in a rocket and shot him into space! Who would do a thing like that?"

Cradling the infant, they stumbled from the crater. "Don't worry," Martha whispered to the child. "We'll tell everyone you're our very own son. The people who did this will never find you! Let's call him Clark, Jonathan! Clark Kent will be such a distinguished-sounding name."

Far away, in a metal vault beneath the earth, a fist encased in a heavy gauntlet began to pound away on the wall before it. Doomsday was coming.

As a tiny child, Clark Kent was like other boys. But as he grew older, he found he could do things no other boy on Earth could. Nothing could hurt him. He could lift heavy objects, like an old pickup truck. He could see through walls. He could even fly.

When Clark was seventeen, Jonathan showed him the rocket that had brought him to Earth.

Clark was stunned. He knew he was different, but this was stranger than he had imagined. Though uncertain of who he was or where he came from, he knew he must use his special powers for humankind. He decided to go out into the world and secretly aid those who needed his help.

Years passed. Inside the underground vault, sharp knuckle-spikes ripped through the creature's tattered glove, as the rhythmic fist-pounding continued.

In Metropolis, a crowd looked up openmouthed as the experimental space plane, the *Constitution*, roared overhead. Suddenly there was a blinding flash.

"Something's happened to the *Constitution*!" someone cried. "It's spinning out of control! It's going to crash!"

Faster than a speeding bullet, Clark leapt into the sky. He soared beneath the fuselage and steadied the plane until it reached the airport runway.

As the plane touched ground, Lois Lane, a reporter for the *Daily Planet*, jumped out. "Who are you?" she cried. "How did you do that?"

But instead of answering, Clark flew away.

The next day, the Metropolis *Daily Planet* ran the headline MYSTERIOUS SUPERMAN SAVES SPACE PLANE.

Clark flew home to his parents. He was worried. People knew about him now. They would be looking for him. How could he continue to do good and still lead a normal life?

Jonathan Kent had an idea. When Clark wanted to make a public appearance, he could wear a costume, a blue one with a red cape. He would wear a shield containing an "S" for "Superman," the name they had called him, on his chest and cape. But in his private life, he could slick back his hair and wear glasses. No one would ever guess Clark Kent was Superman.

Beneath the earth, the pounding continued. The glove began to shred, revealing a massive hand with flesh like weathered granite.

Lois Lane rushed into the *Daily Planet* editorial offices. "Look, Jimmy," she cried, as she waved a sheaf of paper at the red-haired teenage photographer. "I finally got an interview with Superman."

"Gosh, that's great, Miss Lane," said Jimmy Olsen. "I wish I could meet him too!"

Jimmy jumped to his feet to follow Lois as she rushed into the office of Perry White, the paper's managing editor. "Hey, Miss Lane, guess who the Chief just hired?"

But Lois was too busy to listen. "Perry," she cried, "I finally got an interview with Superman!"

"Sorry, Lois, we already have one," said Perry. He held up that morning's edition of the *Daily Planet*. The headline read, THE EXCLUSIVE STORY ON SUPERMAN.

"Here's the guy who beat you to the story," Perry White continued. "Lois Lane, meet our newest reporter, Clark Kent!"

Beneath the earth, the pounding became more incessant as, again and again, the fist's sharp protrusions gouged the sarcophagus walls.

Billionaire Lex Luthor owned many of the businesses and much real estate in Metropolis, so even a party aboard his yacht was considered newsworthy. Lois and Clark were sent to cover it.

While they were aboard Luthor's yacht, it was invaded by terrorists. Superman captured them, and the balding, middle-aged Luthor revealed that he had known about the attack all along and had chosen to do nothing, hoping that Superman would rush to the rescue. Now that he had seen him in action, Luthor wanted Superman to work for him. Superman declined.

The mayor of Metropolis was furious that Luthor would willingly endanger so many people with this scheme. He ordered Superman to carry Lex Luthor off to jail.

From that moment on, Lex Luthor and Superman were enemies. And as time went by, Luthor became more and more jealous of Superman's power in Metropolis, a power that rivaled his own. But despite all Luthor's efforts to destroy Superman, he failed.

Deep underground, repeated mauling raked furrows in the wall of the container. But the metal wall held . . . so far.

Several months later, Clark Kent stood in front of the crater in the field at his parents' house, staring down at the rocket that had brought him to Earth. Suddenly a holographic image of a man in a black bodysuit appeared. In a detached voice, the man called Clark "Kal-El" and revealed he was Clark's real father, Jor-El. He said he and his mother Lara had sent Kal-El to Earth to save him when their planet Krypton was destroyed.

On Earth, Clark learned, he had become like a solar battery. He had absorbed and metabolized the energy of the sun and had powers and abilities far beyond those of mortal men. An energy aura protected him and made him invulnerable to most dangers. He had become the most powerful being on Earth.

As Clark stood, stunned by the newly-revealed origin of his powers, he was caught in an energy web and his mind flooded with images of Krypton. Clark now knew where he came from. But even though he was conceived on Krypton, he was glad that Earth was his home.

The creature's fist pounded with greater intensity. Dents on the wall's surface began to stretch and stress the metal.

Over the next few years, many things changed in Metropolis.

Jimmy Olsen and Superman became friends. Lois Lane and Clark Kent also became friends instead of rivals. And then they fell in love.

Lois and Clark eventually decided to get married. But Clark was worried. He was afraid that if he told Lois the truth about who he really was, she might not want to go through with the wedding. But he knew he loved her too much to lie to her.

Gathering all his courage, Clark Kent told Lois that he led a double life—that in truth he was Superman.

Lois was stunned. She realized that as Superman Clark was often in danger. But she loved him too much to let this stop her from marrying him.

Far beneath the earth, the metal wall shuddered from the incessant pounding. Suddenly, with a crack like thunder, the spiked fist sheared through the wall and hit the rock and clay of the earth beyond. Swiftly the creature's spiked fist began to pound and claw upward to the Earth's surface.

Lex Luthor developed radiation poisoning from a chunk of Kryptonite, a mineral deadly to Superman, which he wore in a ring. Sometime later he died in an airplane crash.

But lawyers going through Lex Luthor's legal papers discovered a secret will, leaving the billionaire's entire fortune to a handsome, red-haired young man in Australia. This man was Lex Luthor's son.

However, no one but Luthor's closest associates knew the truth. Luthor, it turned out, had faked his death. He had had the scientists who worked for him save his brain and genetically grow a new, healthy, *young* body around it. Lex Luthor had returned as his own son.

Even those few associates who knew the truth about the original Lex Luthor came to believe that the young man wasn't evil and corrupt like his father. But Lex Luthor II was biding his time. One day he would defeat Superman, and once again, Metropolis would belong to him.

Beside a mountain lake, the ground cracked and buckled. A flock of crows rose, screeching an alarm as deer leapt in panic through the towering forest. A jagged left hand pounded into the crystal air, as a goggled, manlike being staggered from the hole he had ripped through the earth. He was swaddled like a mummy in olive-colored cloth, his right arm bound behind his back by a thick metal cable.

Doomsday had arrived.

One

The late-afternoon sun gilded Metropolis's sky-scrapers, throwing long purple shadows across the island. But Superman was in no mood to enjoy its beauty. As he flew over the city, he squinted, searching the streets below for the Underworld Renegades.

The Underworlders were originally a group of monsters, created long ago by a mad scientist at a secret government research facility, Project Cadmus. *If the Renegades, a group of Warrior Underworlders, were only monsters,* Superman thought, *they'd be easier to spot.* But he knew that in time homeless humans from the streets of the city had joined the monsters in the vast tunnels carved in the bedrock below Metropolis. Though few of the inhabitants of Underworld were warlike, Superman knew the Renegades were armed and dangerous.

"Pete's falling!"

Superman was jerked from his thoughts by a cry from a half-finished skyscraper. An ironworker was tumbling from one of the upper girders toward the ground far below.

Even as Superman dove to the rescue, another worker grabbed a cable and swung out into the air. The ironworker's muscles rippled and tensed beneath ebony skin as he caught the falling man and hauled him back to safety.

"Henry, man, thanks!" sighed Pete, as Henry Johnson swung him onto the construction platform. But before Henry could join him there, the hook holding his cable slipped. Suddenly it was Henry who was falling.

With a whoosh of air, Superman caught the construction worker. "Superman!" Henry cried. "I thought I was a dead man. I owe you my life!"

"You already saved a man today at great danger to yourself," Superman said. "Just keep on making your life count for something!" Superman lowered Henry to the ground. Then, with a smile and wave, he was gone.

Though Henry waved back, he couldn't make himself smile. *Keep on making my life count for something?* he thought. *Superman wouldn't say that if he knew what a mess I've made of my life so far.*

• • •

Doomsday stood unmoving in an open field. A yellow bird fluttered onto his open palm. For a moment he studied it. Then, with a lightning-swift movement, he closed his fist. The tiny goldfinch gave a single squawk and died. A horrible howl of laughter echoed from beneath the creature's hood.

"Hi, Miss Lane! You've got stuff in your mail slot! See you later!" Jimmy Olsen waved his camera at Lois Lane as he rushed past her and out the swinging doors of the *Daily Planet* press-room.

The Chief probably wants Jimmy to get some shots of the homeless shelter Lex Luthor II is donating to Metropolis. Lex sure is nothing like his father, Lois thought as she pulled a ripped piece of notebook paper from her mail slot.

Lois frowned. Scrawled on the paper were the words: *SEND SUPERMAN TO THE BASEMENT UNDER THE METRO WEST POWER STATION. METROPOLIS IS IN DANGER.* The note was signed, *A FRIEND.*

Clark isn't around. Lois bit her lip as she thought. *And I don't want to leave this note in Clark's mail slot. Someone might see it. Can't let anyone suspect he's Superman.*

An idea hit her, and Lois rushed to Clark's computer. She typed in a coded message, protected by their secret password.

Lois almost bumped into Perry White as she rushed out the swinging doors. "Hi, Chief! When Clark gets back, would you tell him there's a message on his computer?" Then, like a whirlwind, she was gone.

Doomsday stood, hunched and menacing, before an ancient oak. Despite its gnarled and twisted trunk, the tree's golden, autumnal crown proclaimed it king of the forest. With a blow from one hand, Doomsday splintered the oak. Then, felling tree after tree, he began to smash a path through the forest.

So far, Superman's search for the Renegades had been in vain. As the sun set, he landed beside the giant globe that decorated the top of the *Daily Planet* Building. He entered the structure through a service door and, at superspeed, changed into his business suit as he rushed down fifteen flights of stairs to the newsroom.

"Hi, Clark," said Perry White. "About time you got back. Lois left a message on your computer."

Clark flipped on his computer. Seconds after the message appeared, the screen blinked and died. The lights in the building faded, leaving the newsroom in inky blackness.

Below the Metro West Power Station, the Renegades cheered. They had stolen Metropolis electricity. "Power to Underworld!" they cried. "Power to Underworld!"

Like a column of granite, Doomsday stood beside a freeway. Now and again a car would approach, blinding him with its headlights. Then the car would zip past to mount the long ramp that led to the top of an overpass. Doomsday stepped onto the freeway. He came up to one of the bridge supports. Wrapping an arm around it, he tugged. The overpass toppled, crushing passing cars. Then, laughing like a crack of thunder, Doomsday leapt into the starlit sky.

Metropolis at night usually sparkled like a mound of glittering jewels. Tonight it was dark, but not silent. Horns blared at intersections. Police sirens screamed. Far overhead, Superman soared like a rocket. Lois's message said an anonymous tip had warned her of danger to Metropolis and that she would meet him at the Metro West Power Station. Superman worried that Lois might have walked into a trap.

Suddenly, his superhearing registered a high-pitched whine coming from beneath the city. *Somehow the Renegades are behind this*, Superman thought. *But what are they up to*?

Superman dove into a sewer conduit and flew

through a series of interconnected tunnels. Deep into the Underworld he sped, coming ever closer to the source of the sound.

Suddenly, the whine became a banshee wail. A huge whirling blade sliced up through the tunnel beneath him. *It looks like a giant drill*, thought Superman. *It must be powered by electricity diverted from Metropolis. But why is it here?*

Superman grabbed the blade. The motor revved ineffectually as Superman shoved the drill backward through the hole it had bored in the bedrock.

The drill crashed and shattered onto the floor of a vast cavern. Beyond it, an army of war machines waited. Superman was amazed. The drill was carving a tunnel. The Renegades planned to invade Metropolis! Bullets bounced off Superman's chest as the Renegades opened fire. But one by one, Superman captured them. With his heat vision, he melted the war machines into useless slag.

"You have us," the Renegades' leader mumbled through his tusks. "But we have lady reporter captive! Old Charlie gonna kill her dead 'fore you can reach her!"

Superman grabbed the leader by the throat. "Where is she?" he growled.

Following the Renegade's directions, Superman smashed his way through solid rock. In a small cavern lit by lanterns, he tackled a gray-haired man holding a .44 Magnum.

Suddenly, from a dark corner, Lois called out, "Superman! Don't hurt him! Charlie's the one who sent the note that warned us of the Renegades' attack!"

Superman dropped Charlie. He was glad to see that Lois was alive.

Charlie climbed to his feet, brushing dust from his clothes. "I lived here in Underworld for quite a while," Charlie began. "And I knew most of the folks here wanted peace, same as me. So I pretended to join the Renegades so I could find out their plan. When I found out what they were up to, I knew we'd need you, Superman. Miss Lane had been kind to me when I was panhandlin'. Used to give me donuts on her way to work. So I sent the note to her 'cause I wanted her to get the story. And I knew she'd tell you. I just didn't think she'd come and get herself captured. Good thing I was able to convince 'em to let me be her executioner."

Under Charlie's supervision, the Underworlders jailed the Renegades. Superman offered to help Charlie and his friends join the surface world, but Charlie refused.

"I can't get a job up there, and I'm human," Charlie said. "Who's gonna hire a bunch of freaks and monsters like my friends here. Thanks anyway, but there's nothin' for us on the surface world."

Charlie and Lois shook hands. Then Superman lifted Lois into his arms and flew through the twisting tunnels toward the surface.

"Charlie's more than paid me back for a few donuts," Lois said. "I just hope he and his friends will be safe here in Underworld."

Ignoring the roar of traffic, Doomsday strode across a highway. A horn blared frantically as a truck driver tried to warn the creature to get out of the way. Doomsday whirled and grabbed the truck's front grill. With one hand tied behind his back, he flipped the rig on its side. Skidding to avoid an impact, the driver of another rig radioed for help. The monster was headed east.

Two

The sophomore civics class of George Washington High in Easton, Ohio, stared at a television propped on the teacher's desk.

"The interview you'll be watching is taking place in Metropolis, for the benefit of schools nationwide," said Mr. Swanson. "I want you all to pay attention."

The interviewer, a newswoman named Cat Grant, introduced Superman, the Man of Steel, who answered questions about his accomplishments. He spoke about how the use of force was sometimes necessary in the war against crime.

In the back of the classroom, a boy with long, light brown hair wearing a backward baseball cap shifted restlessly. "That guy is such a dork!" he mumbled.

Suddenly, the broadcast was interrupted by an emergency news bulletin—a Doomsday monster was destroying an oil refinery in western Ohio.

When the interview program returned, Superman was gone. Cat Grant explained that Superman had left to stop the Doomsday monster, and that the interview would be concluded at another time.

The bell rang, signaling the end of school. The long-haired boy scooped up his books and stomped out of the classroom. "Just got up and left in the middle of an interview!" he mumbled. "Can you believe that jerk?"

"Gimme a break, Mitch. He decided to help people, instead of flapping his lip. Why does that make him a jerk?" Mitch's friend asked.

"It's just . . . he sounds too good to be true," Mitch sighed. "Nobody's that perfect."

Half an hour later, Mitch slammed the door as he walked into his house. "Is that you, Mitch?" called his mom, as she heated baby formula over a gas burner. In her high chair nearby, little Becky banged on her tray with a wooden spoon.

"No, it's the Frankenstein monster himself," Mitch snarled. "And don't ask about the Superweasel on TV. He was called away on some case and bailed out early."

Mitch hung on the open door of the refrigerator, gazing sullenly inside. "How come there's never any soda around this house? Dad always has soda for me at his new apartment!"

Mitch's mom was annoyed. "Your sister was sick and I wasn't able to get out. I do the best I can, but I'm not perfect."

Mitch stomped toward the kitchen door. "Jeez," he snarled. "No wonder dad wants a divorce! I—"

The rest of his sentence was drowned out by the screech of twisting metal and broken glass as their old 1986 Ford came crashing through the kitchen wall. Mitch pulled his mom back as the oven was wrenched from the wall and overturned by the impact.

Mitch peered around the wreckage. A monster swathed in olive cloth with one hand tied behind his back took one menacing step toward their house, then another.

"Something tells me that's the Doomsday monster Superman went to stop. Looks like the Superjerk blew it. Figures!" Mitch cried. "Get Becky, Mom. We gotta get out of here!"

As Mitch's mother lifted the baby into her arms, Doomsday shattered the kitchen door. But before he could step inside, Superman landed in front of him, blocking his entrance.

The monster slammed Superman with his fist, trying to knock him aside, but the Man of Steel didn't budge. Doomsday was startled. Never before had he met with such resistance.

Superman smelled gas. "The Doomsday monster must have ruptured a gas line!" he gasped. "I've got to end this fight fast!"

But as Superman tried to grab Doomsday, the monster kicked him in the stomach. Superman was knocked backward through the walls of the house and into an elm that grew in the side yard. He shook his head dazedly. He didn't think he had ever been hit that hard.

Hearing a cry for help, Superman struggled to his feet and flew through the house. As Doomsday reached Mitch's mom, Superman blasted the creature back with the enormous power of his heat vision.

As the heat blast washed over Doomsday, the monster gave a grunt of surprise. The temperature was so intense it melted the mask from the right half of his face and body, revealing skin the color and texture of hewn stone, covered with bony spikes. The cable that bound his right arm began to glow white-hot.

Doomsday tugged mightily against the cable. Suddenly it broke. His right arm was finally free. Even as Doomsday lifted both fists with a roar of triumph, a tremendous explosion ripped through the air.

Mitch, safe from the blast, saw Doomsday leap into the air. Superman flew after him. Then, from

within the burning house, Mitch heard his baby sister Becky's cry.

Mitch climbed through the burning timbers and snatched little Becky into his arms. "Mom," he called. "Mom, are you in there? Are you okay?" But his mom lay on the ground, unconscious, surrounded by flames. He couldn't carry her out and the baby too.

"Help!" Mitch cried, as loud as he could. "Superman! Please! You gotta come back! You gotta save us!"

Even as Mitch called out again, he was worried. *What if Doomsday is beating Superman? What will we do then*?

As Superman tackled Doomsday in midair, he heard Mitch's desperate cry. With telescopic vision, he glanced back toward Mitch's house.

Oh, no, Superman thought. *They're trapped! I saw the blast blow the boy free. I thought the others were free as well!*

As Superman struggled with the creature, he worried. If he stopped fighting Doomsday to save Mitch's family, the monster would then be free to hurt more people. He knew he couldn't let Mitch's family die. But he also couldn't let Doomsday go free.

Far below was a large lake. This gave Superman an idea. He grabbed Doomsday around the neck and dragged him down from the sky, deep into the lake's muddy floor, burying him upside down to his waist. Surely this would give Superman the time he needed to free Mitch's family.

Mitch was hoarse from breathing smoke. Still, he held his little sister and croaked out once again, "Superman, save us!"

And suddenly, Superman was there. He scooped up Mitch's mom with one arm and Mitch and the baby with the other. And then, to Mitch's relief, they were soaring above the flames.

"Superman, you saved us!" cried Mitch.

"Glad I was able to help, son," said Superman as he lowered them to the ground far from the flames. In the distance, they could hear fire engines coming to fight the blaze.

"Doomsday's still out there," Superman said.

"Go on, Superman. I know you have to stop him. And don't worry," said Mitch. "I'll take care of Mom and Becky until help arrives. You know, I used to think . . ." And then Mitch stopped. How could he tell Superman he used to think he was a phony?

"Never mind," Mitch finally said. "Just . . . good luck."

"Thanks. I might need it," said Superman. In an instant he was high in the air. Then he was out of sight.

. . .

Outside the Kirby County Police Station many miles away, Doomsday, wet and covered with lake slime, landed atop a police car, crushing it. But Superman was right behind him.

He rammed into the creature feetfirst, half-burying him in the pavement. But Doomsday kicked Superman back.

Suddenly bullets were falling like rain around the combatants. Overhead, a group of military choppers circled, guns blazing. The U.S. Army had arrived.

Their bullets didn't seem to hurt Doomsday any more than they would Superman. But the gunfire did make the creature angry.

Doomsday leapt to his feet. With a roar, he ripped a street sign from the sidewalk. Then he hurled it like a spear through one of the hovering helicopters.

The chopper's motor made a grinding sound. The blades quit turning, and the chopper plummeted toward the ground. Superman snatched the pilots from their seats seconds before the chopper crashed into the town hall, then set them down safely.

Several blocks away, Doomsday was smashing the pumps at the corner gas station. Gasoline spewed from the destroyed pumps like a fountain.

Superman dived for Doomsday, but this time the creature was ready for him. Laughing with abandon, Doomsday ripped up a streetlight and swung it at Superman like a baseball bat. A spark from the streetlight's wiring ignited the spewing gasoline.

The explosion leveled the block and blew Superman and Doomsday in opposite directions. Superman was buried under tons of shattered concrete. He had a finite amount of energy, and it was slowly being depleted. He had never been in a fight like this before. What would happen if his energy ran out?

What seemed like hours but was really only minutes later, Superman shoved the rubble aside and staggered to his feet. He looked around, dismayed.

Main Street was destroyed. And Doomsday was gone.

At Metropolis Heliport, Lois Lane and Jimmy Olsen, lugging his camera, rushed for the *Daily Planet* news chopper. It waited, blades revolving slowly, as they climbed aboard. Then, like a hovering dragonfly, it rose to join the swarm of other helicopters racing to cover the fight of the century.

Superman flew east at top speed, scanning the landscape below. *I've never seen anything equal to Doomsday for sheer brute strength,* he thought. *Or rage. There's no pattern to his destruction. He seems to wander from place to place, attacking whatever catches his eye!*

Below him, a collapsed highway swarmed with rescue workers. Doomsday had been here. But the creature moved in ten-mile leaps, at half the speed of sound. *Where is he now?* Superman wondered.

He scanned the area with his telescopic vision. He spotted overturned cars and smashed windows at the Midvale Plaza Shopping Center. Doomsday was there.

At the LexCorp Building in Metropolis, Lex Luthor II answered the telephone. "What do you mean, a Doomsday creature is destroying my Lex-Mart store in Midvale? I thought Superman had gone to stop that monster!"

A beautiful blond young woman ran into the room. "What is it, Lex?" she asked. "Is Superman in trouble?" As she ran, the ruffled dress she wore changed shape, becoming a red and blue costume much like Superman's. "I came to Earth from my world, and took this human form, to be as much like Superman as I could," she said. As the shape-shifter turned toward the balcony, the glass windows swung open. "Superman's the best man I know, next to you, Lex. If he's in trouble, I have to help him!"

Lex reached out a hand to stop her before she could fly off into the air. "Listen to me, Supergirl," he said. "Superman can handle that monster! Trust me. But if Doomsday does break free again, he may come this way. Superman would want you to stay in Metropolis, to protect the city that he loves."

Inside the Midvale Lex-Mart, a giant TV screen showed a professional wrestler called Major Mayhem. Major called out, "Hey, you! I'm talking to you! Come closer! You don't want to miss a single moment of the greatest spectacle in the history of professional wrestling."

As Doomsday stepped closer, Major Mayhem promised a wrestling slugfest in Metropolis Arena. He asked the audience, "Now where you gonna go?"

A sign flashed the name "Metropolis Arena," as the audience screamed, *"Metropolis! Metropolis Arena! Metropolis!"*

For the first time, Doomsday spoke. "Mhh-trr-plsss?" he repeated.

Superman zoomed in through the Lex-Mart's smashed windows, past overturned racks and shopping carts. He tackled Doomsday, tumbling him through the wall and into the parking lot.

News choppers circled overhead. In the lead chopper, bearing the *Daily Planet* logo, Jimmy Olsen pointed his camera at Doomsday. "Wow, he's a big one!" said Jimmy.

Very big! thought Lois. *Please, Clark, be careful,* she prayed.

But Lois had a job to do. Using the chopper's radio, she reported to the *Daily Planet* what was happening.

Down below, Doomsday hurled a parked bus at Superman, knocking him through a store window. A sign that said METROPOLIS, 60 MILES caught Doomsday's eye. He stared at the sign as though in thought.

Finally he growled, "Mhh-trr-plsss!" and leapt into the air.

As Superman struggled from the wreckage, he knew that Doomsday had recognized the word *Metropolis* from the wrestling commercial. Doomsday would reach the city of Metropolis in six leaps. And there was no way Superman could stop him in time.

Three

Doomsday's sixth leap carried him to a construction site in western Metropolis. Superman caught up with him there. He lifted Doomsday high over the city, rocketing him past hovering news choppers and toward the vacuum of space.

Lois Lane was worried, but Jimmy reassured her as he took another series of photographs. "Superman will be all right! After all, he's Superman!"

From his office at Project Cadmus, the secret government research facility, a horned telepath called Dubbilex closed his eyes and reached out to Doomsday with his mind. Dubbilex was worried. In the past, Project Cadmus had constructed creatures like himself and the Underworlders. *Could Cadmus have secretly created Doomsday as well?* he wondered.

As he read Doomsday's mind, Dubbilex felt a

moment of panic. There was nothing there but rage and destruction.

Dubbilex attacked Doomsday with a telepathic mind-bolt, but it had no effect. *Doomsday will have to be stopped by physical force,* he thought, *or not at all.*

At the Kents' farm, Martha and Jonathan Kent watched the battle between Superman and Doomsday on television.

Martha was angry. "That's our son," she said. "He's being beaten to a pulp and those reporters are treating the fight like it's a sporting event."

But Jonathan reassured her. "Clark is our boy, but to the world he's Superman. The reporters don't mean to be cruel. They just don't think anything bad can happen to him."

As he said the words, he thought to himself, *I only hope they're right.*

The battle raged through Metropolis. Although Superman was tiring, he continued to fight Doomsday. But again and again, the creature slammed him to the ground.

Henry Johnson, the construction worker Superman had saved, stood on a girder high over Metropolis. Looking down, he saw that Superman was in trouble.

With no thought for his own safety, Henry swung to the ground. He owed Superman his life, and he meant to repay him. He snatched up a sledgehammer and raced toward the combatants. But he feared it would take more than a hammer's blow to fell the monster.

Doomsday had seen plenty of explosions. And he had learned how to cause them. At the construction site, he deliberately ripped through a gas main, then kicked out at an electrical conduit. The explosion blew the combatants sky-high, destroying the construction site and burying Henry Johnson in its rubble.

Rocked by the powerful blast, the LexCorp Building shuddered and shook as its windows shattered, splashing shards of glass across the carpet of Lex Luthor's office.

Inside, Supergirl ran toward the shattered window. "I think Doomsday may be more than Superman can handle alone! Don't be annoyed, Lex, but I have to go help him!"

Lex was shaken. The fight seemed to be going badly, and much of Metropolis had been destroyed. Reluctantly, Lex agreed that Supergirl should go to Superman's aid. Supergirl leapt into the air and took off after the Man of Steel and the creature called Doomsday.

Meanwhile, amid smoke and flames, Superman tackled Doomsday and dragged him into the air where, he hoped, Doomsday could do no more harm. But Doomsday wasn't ready to give up. He raked Superman with his arm-spikes, ripping a gash in the Man of Steel's powerful chest.

Superman gasped in agony. Until now, his energy aura had protected him, and he had been victorious in the battles he had fought. He had confronted Doomsday, almost certain of his eventual triumph. Now he wasn't sure he could stop the creature.

Then Doomsday raised his fist and smashed Superman with a shattering blow that hurled him unconscious to the ground.

Doomsday roared with victory.

On a rooftop nearby, one of Superman's friends, the inventor Professor Hamilton, stood beside an old ex-boxer named Bibbo. Next to them was a huge laser cannon. They looked up at Doomsday with amazement.

"What kinda creature is strong enough to defeat Superman?" Bibbo wondered.

"A very powerful one," said Professor Hamilton. "But maybe we can stop him! Quick, help me aim the laser cannon!"

But before Professor Hamilton could get the falling monster in the cross hairs of the laser gun, Supergirl tackled Doomsday in midair.

Doomsday was surprised but not worried. He slammed her with his spiked fists.

The blow was so hard that as Supergirl hit the ground, she reverted to her claylike, near protoplasmic natural form. The shape-shifter lay in the gutter and didn't move.

From the rooftop below, Professor Hamilton roared, "Now!" as he pulled the trigger of his laser cannon. The laser blast hit Doomsday square in the middle of his back. Doomsday was hurt, and he roared angrily as he fell.

The monster landed so hard he broke through the street. Below him were more of Metropolis's buried gas mains and electrical wires. Deliberately, Doomsday ripped through them.

As this second explosion rocked Metropolis, Superman, broken and bloody, staggered to his feet. In the distance he heard gunfire. Gathering his waning strength, the Man of Steel leapt into the air and flew toward the sound.

Down below, Doomsday was stalking through a rain of police bullets as if he didn't feel them. A line of policemen blocked the road directly ahead of him.

Doomsday grabbed a cop named Maggie Sawyer by the neck and hurled her high into the air. Superman dived and caught her in his arms before she crashed into the ground.

"That monster's too much for any of you to handle, Lieutenant!" Superman said. "Get the other police away from here, on the double."

Once again, Superman tackled Doomsday. As they struggled against each other, shock troops from Cadmus Research, wearing flight suits, soared into the air above them.

"Project Cadmus said our shock cannons should stop that monster!" said one soldier.

"But they keep moving," said another. "What if our cannon fire hits Superman instead?"

"That's a chance we'll have to take," said the Guardian, their commander and security chief, as they opened fire. "Seems like even Superman can't stop that monster!"

In front of the *Daily Planet* Building, amid a rain of cannon fire, Superman and Doomsday fought toe-to-toe. Doomsday's fists were like hammers, pounding Superman into the pavement. Superman's arms felt heavy as lead, but he braced his feet and concentrated on returning blow for blow. *Even if it kills me,* thought Superman, *this is where I hold the line.*

The *Daily Planet* news chopper hovered nearby. As Doomsday grabbed Superman by the throat and slammed him against the pavement, Lois Lane held her breath. *Superman is battered and bleeding,* she thought. She had never seen him like this. How could he keep fighting when he could hardly stand?

Suddenly, the monster flung Superman into the air, slamming his body into the *Daily Planet* helicopter. The chopper began to spin out of control.

Alarmed, Superman spun around and grabbed the helicopter. He steadied it as he lowered it to the ground. All the while, Jimmy Olsen shot picture after picture of Doomsday's rampage.

"Doomsday's shrugging off that cannon fire like it was nothing!" said Jimmy. "He seems to be unstoppable!"

Lois leapt from the chopper and ran to Superman. She begged him to retreat, to wait for help. But Superman knew that if he hesitated, more lives would be lost.

Hidden by obscuring smoke, Superman kissed Lois as if for the last time. "Just remember," he said, "no matter what happens, I will always love you."

Then, with a roar of anger and resolve, Superman leapt from Lois's arms. He tackled Doomsday headfirst, smashing him into an abandoned bus. But again Doomsday slammed him back. With fury and determination, he pounded Superman into the street, burying him in rubble.

Lois saw Superman driven into the ground. "He's in trouble," she cried. "I have to help him!"

Lois ran forward, shouting and waving her arms, hoping to distract Doomsday and give Superman time to recover. Doomsday was puzzled. He took a step toward Lois, past the mound of rubble where Superman was buried. Then he took another step.

Up through the rubble, Superman launched himself at Doomsday. "Lois, get back!" he warned. Desperately, he slammed Doomsday, first with his weakened fists, then with the blazing force of his heat vision.

Superman had sworn never to take a life. But could he stop Doomsday without killing him? Or could he kill Doomsday, he wondered, even if he wanted to?

Toe-to-toe, the behemoths fought, the force of their blows shattering windows in the surrounding buildings. Superman realized that to stop Doomsday he would have to be as ferocious and unrelenting as the monster himself.

Superman knew that he had enough strength left for one final blow. With every ounce of his remaining energy, he slammed Doomsday, even as Doomsday raked him with an uppercut that snapped his head back.

Doomsday staggered and fell. Then Superman swayed and fell beside him.

Lois ran to Superman. She threw herself down beside him and gathered her loved one gently into her arms. "Please be alive," she whispered. "Please, please be alive."

Half the country away, Lois's prayer was echoed by Clark's parents, who stared at the television with tears rolling down their cheeks. "Please, please let our son be alive!"

One by one, people began to creep from the buildings, staring awestruck at the defeated monster and their fallen hero—the man they had always thought was invulnerable.

As Jimmy Olsen snapped the final photos, Lois Lane clung to Superman, begging him to hang on until the paramedics arrived.

"Doomsday . . . is he . . . is he . . . ?" Superman whispered hoarsely.

"He's down. You stopped him!" Lois clutched Superman to her. "You saved us all."

Metropolis was saved. The victory, Superman thought, had been worth the sacrifice. With a sigh he closed his eyes. Then the last spark of a life that had burned bright with heroism flickered and died.

Four

Lois clung to Superman's body as a corps of paramedics leapt from ambulances. "Please," she said, "you've got to help him!" She stepped back to give them room.

A paramedic felt for Superman's pulse. "There's nothing," he said.

The horned telepath Dubbilex, arriving on a Cadmus antigravity platform, scanned Superman's mind, then shook his head. "There is no brain wave activity."

"How can you be sure?" Lois cried. "Superman is an alien! His body differs from ours!"

Cat Grant, the newswoman, rushed from the newly landed WGBS news chopper. "As harsh as this sounds, Lois, we've got to face facts," she said. "I'm afraid it's true."

But Lois refused to listen. Tears rolled down her

cheeks as she pleaded, "We owe Superman more than we can ever repay him! We've got to try to revive him!"

The police and paramedics agreed. They placed two defibrillator paddles on Superman's chest and sent a strong jolt of electricity coursing through his body. But the jolts had no effect.

As the paramedics worked to revive Superman, a man in a trench coat climbed from the cab of a large covered transport displaying the distinctive Cadmus logo. Cadmus workers fitted Doomsday's body with antigravity discs and lifted it onto their shoulders.

Police Lieutenant Maggie Sawyer stopped them. "What authorization do you have to take that monster's body?" she asked.

"I'm Director Westfield, and Project Cadmus is authorized to take all alien bodies. Doomsday's . . . and Superman's!" he snarled.

But Maggie Sawyer refused. "Until I have that authorization in writing from the President himself, you're not taking anything!"

Maggie turned to the Guardian, Cadmus's security chief. "I wonder if the energy from your power platform could be used to augment the defibrillators," she said. "If we can run enough energy through Superman's body, maybe we can get his heart beating again!"

"Had the same idea myself," puffed a voice from behind her. "Got here as fast as we could."

Maggie Sawyer and the Guardian turned. Professor Hamilton and Bibbo staggered toward them, lugging a machine covered with plugs and sockets. "This is an energy collection unit," said Professor Hamilton. "It will channel the shock cannons' beams into the defibrillator paddles."

Soon the Guardian was hovering in the air above the unit as Bibbo held the paddles to Superman's chest.

"Are you sure you want to do this?" asked Professor Hamilton. "A lot of electricity is going to course through those paddles. You could get hurt!"

Bibbo nodded grimly. "I gotta do it. It might help Superman. And if things go bad, no one'll miss a pug like me. Blast away!"

"Thank you," said Professor Hamilton. Then he gave the order. "Now!"

The Guardian fired beams of energy from his shock cannons into the unit. A jolt of power ran through the paddles. There was a crack like thunder, and Bibbo flew into the air. He landed on his back with a loud thud. "Is . . . is Superman . . . better?" he croaked.

"It didn't work," Professor Hamilton sighed.

"I concur," said Dubbilex sadly. "There is no brain activity. Superman is truly dead."

Sobbing, Lois clutched Superman's torn cape.

A WGBS news van roared up. Technicians jumped out with cameras and sound units. "Okay, Miss Grant," said the cameraman. "We're ready when you are!"

Cat gave Lois a little shake. "You've got to snap out of it," she said. "You're a good reporter! This story needs to be told—as only you can tell it! We've all got our jobs to do!"

Lois brushed the tears from her eyes. "You're right, Cat," she said bravely. "Come on, Jimmy. We'd better get to the *Planet*."

Several blocks away, Lex Luthor II lifted the body of the near-protoplasmic shape-shifter called Supergirl from the gutter. She opened her eyes and started to struggle. "Lex!" she croaked. "I have to help Superman."

Only her eyes are the same, Luthor thought. *In this form, her body looks like charred wood.* "No one can help Superman, love," Luthor said, holding her tightly as he climbed into the back of his limousine. "He's dead . . . but you're alive! Now show some spirit! Use your shape-changing powers to mend yourself. I want my Supergirl back!"

She closed her eyes. "It . . . it is difficult." She clenched her fist as burning pain engulfed her. "But for you I would move mountains!" She bit her lip in agony as her features shifted and her human beauty was restored.

As Supergirl rested limply against the lush leather seat, Lex took a bottle from the bar and casually poured himself a drink. "Amazing," he murmured. "Simply amazing."

The *Daily Planet* newsroom was quiet as a morgue. People clustered around portable TV sets as the non-stop coverage of the events surrounding Superman's death continued.

Jimmy handed a pile of photographs to Perry White.

Perry stared at them solemnly. "These are good, Jimmy," he said. "Maybe the best you've ever taken."

"I know," mumbled Jimmy. "But using them seems like exploiting the death of a friend."

"I understand how you feel," Perry said reassuringly. "But we're still journalists, and we've got a paper to publish. These photos will remind the world of Superman's sacrifice. Look at how Lois is handling this. You know how she felt about Superman. And her fiancé Clark is among the hundreds missing. But she hasn't let it stop her from doing her job."

Lois sat at her desk. Dashing the tears from her eyes, she typed the last words of her story, then handed it to Perry. "I . . . I guess I never thought Superman could die," she said.

"Superman may be dead," said Jimmy, trying to cheer her up, "but Mr. Kent will turn up. You know how lucky he's always been!"

But Lois knew better. When Superman died, Clark Kent's luck ran out.

In the poorest section of Metropolis, known as Hob's Bay, the old ex-boxer Bibbo stood outside his run-down bar, the Ace o' Clubs. He stared glumly at the lowering clouds.

Suddenly a streak of blue and red arced across the sky. *It's Superman!* Bibbo thought. *He's alive after all!* For a moment, he felt light-headed with joy. Then he saw the figure's golden hair. It was only Supergirl, he realized. His shoulders slumped dejectedly, and with a sigh, he went inside. He'd already sent his regular customers home, and the bar was deserted. Suddenly tears flooded his eyes and ran in rivulets down his weathered cheeks.

Falling to his knees, he bent his head in prayer. "God? I gotta ask ya . . . why? Why should Superman die . . . when a washed-up ol' roughneck like me goes on livin'? It ain't right, God . . . it just ain't right."

. . .

During the days before Superman's burial, Lex Luthor's office in the LexCorp Building was the calm eye in a storm of activity. Luthor himself supervised every detail of Superman's funeral. He chose the coffin, commissioned the memorial statue, even donated the crypt in Centennial Park.

Try as I might, I couldn't kill Superman, he thought. *But I'm sure going to bury him.*

Lois Lane stood beneath the giant globe that decorated the roof of the *Daily Planet* Building. Wind whipped her trench coat, and rain mixed with her tears. It was as if the heavens themselves were mourning Superman's death.

She stared at the sky, half-expecting Superman to drop from the rolling clouds and land beside her, as he had so many times before. But all the wishes in the world couldn't bring him back.

"Clark died and I couldn't help him," she sighed to herself. "All I could do was report the story. I couldn't even bring myself to call Clark's parents and tell Ma and Pa how sorry I am . . . and admit . . . that Clark's life . . . is over."

Far below, Lois could hear the drums of the funeral procession. With slumped shoulders she went downstairs. Jimmy had said he would be waiting for her

outside on the sidewalk. They would view the funeral procession together.

The crowd was ten rows deep, but Jimmy had saved a place for Lois in front, next to Perry White. They stood in the drizzle, watching the horse-drawn wagon carry Superman's flag-draped coffin toward Centennial Park. Behind it marched the honor guard, firemen, and the police, along with other dignitaries gathered to pay their respects.

All around Lois, Jimmy, and Perry, people turned to one another, eager to share the stories of the times when Superman had helped them or someone they knew. He was their hero. He belonged to all of them.

Lois stared at the casket as it passed. *It can't end like this,* she thought. *I can't just stand on the sidelines and let Clark go.*

Lois wasn't the only one who felt that way. As Superman's casket rolled past, the crowd stepped from the sidewalk and into the street, spontaneously following the coffin. Lois fell in line and joined them.

As they marched through the city, more and more people joined the procession. It seemed that everyone in Metropolis wanted to be at Superman's funeral.

Lois, Jimmy, and Perry tried to stay together, but as the crowd began to funnel into Centennial Park, they were forced apart. One man bumped into another, who angrily shoved someone else. The shoving match soon became a brawl.

At the Kents' farm, Jonathan and Martha sat on the worn sofa. Martha wrung her apron as she stared into the television screen. "It doesn't seem right, us not being there," she said.

"They're burying him with full hero's honors. Even the heads of some countries couldn't get seats there, Martha," Jonathan said for what seemed like the hundredth time. "Nobody knows we're his parents. They wouldn't let us anywhere near him."

"But they're making a circus of that funeral. Where's the dignity in that?" Martha said through her tears.

Jonathan put his arm around her. "Martha," he said, "let's turn that TV off. Let Metropolis say good-bye to Superman in its own way. We'll say good-bye to our son in *our* own way, here on the farm."

In Metropolis, order was restored, and the funeral proceeded. The podium before the crypt was crowded with the heads of nations. Giant TV screens erected around the park showed the President of the United States as he praised Superman, not for his special powers, but for the nobility and goodness with which he had used them.

Meanwhile, in the middle of a shorn wheat field on their farm in Smallville, Kansas, Jonathan and Martha Kent stood before the impact crater made by the rocket that had carried their adopted son to Earth. In her hands Martha held a box containing some of Clark's special things.

Jonathan stood before the hole and spoke to their son. "Here's where the rocket brought you to Earth," he began. "I'll never forget how amazed I was to see you there."

"I reached in . . . and lifted you into my arms," said Martha. "We didn't know where you came from . . . and we didn't care. You were ours, the sweetest little baby in the universe, our gift from heaven. And right from the start, we loved you with all our hearts."

Martha placed Clark's special things in the hole. "Heaven gave you to us," she said, "and now heaven has taken you."

Jonathan plunged his shovel into the crusty earth and hurled dirt into the crater. They buried Clark's things, since they could not bury their son. It was all they could do . . . and it felt empty.

I feel like there's nobody who needs us anymore, thought Jonathan. *Like there's no reason to go on living.* He clutched his chest as he and

Martha trudged disconsolately home through the barren fields.

In Centennial Park, the sorrowful crowd gaped as the giant TV screens showed the burial inside the mausoleum. Slowly, reverently, Superman's coffin was lowered into the crypt. There was not a dry eye in the crowd as all those watching said good-bye to Superman in their own way.

As Martha and Jonathan opened the kitchen door, the phone was ringing urgently. Martha snatched up the receiver.

"It's Lois," she whispered to Jonathan with her hand over the receiver. "Poor child. Sounds like she's been crying."

In a phone booth in Centennial Park, Lois stood, shoulders hunched, trying to block out the noise of the solemnly milling crowd.

"I'm sorry I haven't called before. I just . . . couldn't. Couldn't believe it was true . . . that he's really dead. I asked myself what could I say to you?" Lois fought back the tears. "How can you forgive me? I was there . . . all the time Clark fought Doomsday . . . and all I could do was report the story . . . and watch him die. I couldn't do anything . . . but watch him die."

"Listen to me, Lois," said Jonathan. "It's not your fault. You did all you could. Everyone did everything they could!"

"We're coming, sweetie," Martha said. "Hold on a little while, we'll be right there." Lois needed them, they realized. But the Kents also realized they needed Lois.

Five

Rain mixed with sleet stung Lois's cheeks as she trudged down Clinton Street, past the corner newsstand, past the doorman, and into the lobby of Clark's apartment building.

She rode the elevator to the fifteenth floor, where Martha and Jonathan Kent would be waiting for her. They'd come to Metropolis to clean out Clark's apartment and cancel his lease. Like Lois, they knew he wouldn't be coming back.

Lois opened the door with trembling fingers. *This is the last time I'll ever come here,* she thought. Fighting back tears, she called out, "Martha? Jonathan?"

"We're here, sweetie!" called Martha. Rushing from the bedroom, she took Lois in her arms.

A long-haired boy wearing a backward red baseball cap climbed off the bus from Ohio, carrying a worn backpack and clutching a torn newspaper in one hand.

He pushed his way down the crowded escalator onto the street and out into the teeming lunch-hour crowd. He looked around with a sinking feeling. Metropolis was bigger than he had imagined. "Mitch, old boy," he said to himself, "if you want to be there on time, you better ask directions!"

In Centennial Park, Mitch stood beneath the trees as an icy rain stung his cheeks and soaked his jacket.

On the band shell, a slender woman in a pink suit faced a group of bored-looking reporters. "I'm Mrs. Superman," she declared. "We kept our relationship secret . . ." The woman continued her story, but the reporters looked like all they wanted to do was get out of the rain.

As Mitch watched, a red-haired photographer turned away without taking a single picture. Mitch stepped forward and touched his elbow.

"Excuse me," said Mitch, "but that woman . . . she's not really Mrs. Superman, is she?"

The red-haired man looked at Mitch. "Why do you want to know?"

Mitch held out a sodden Ohio newspaper. Circled in red was an article announcing that Superman's widow was going to make an important announcement in Centennial Park today.

"Look, my name's Jimmy Olsen," the photographer said. "That woman is just another fraud who's trying to exploit Superman's death. There've been a lot of them. I was sent to cover this, but I've seen enough."

The boy looked wet and hungry, Jimmy thought. And very disappointed. "You came all the way from Ohio for this? Why?"

"I . . . I wanted to tell her how sorry I am he died. And how it . . . was all my fault," Mitch finished his sentence in a rush.

"Your fault?" asked Jimmy, puzzled. "Listen, you had anything to eat?"

Mitch hung his head. "I just got off the bus and . . . I'm kinda broke," he said.

"Then the chow is on me," said Jimmy with a grin. "Long as you can handle lunch with me and my pal Bibbo."

Sleet tapped like fingernails against the window of the Hob's Bay Grille. Inside, Bibbo, Jimmy, and Mitch sat in a booth covered in frayed plastic. Their jackets, hung on hooks, dripped puddles onto the worn linoleum floor.

A gray-haired waitress brought a tray loaded with double cheeseburgers, extra-large fries, and chocolate shakes.

Between bites, Mitch told Jimmy and Bibbo how Superman had fought Doomsday, and then, when Mitch called him, had turned back from his battle to save Mitch's mother and baby sister.

"Superman might have been able to stop Doomsday then and there, if it wasn't for me. If it wasn't for me, he might still be alive."

Mitch shoved his food away. Thinking about what he'd done had ruined his appetite. "I used to think Superman was a real dork. I was even joking with one of my friends about it earlier . . . the day he died. I . . . I jinxed him!" Mitch rested his chin on his fist glumly. "What's really weird is . . . my old man ditched us months ago. And then a complete stranger comes along and saves us. Superman died fighting for us! That's why I snuck off to Metropolis. I wanted to talk to his widow . . . to apologize!"

Bibbo reached across the table and patted Mitch's shoulder with a hand the size of a ham. "I understand how you feel, kid," he said. "But far as we know, Superman didn't have no family. But *you* do . . . and I bet your ma's worried sick about you! Superman wouldn't like you worrying her like that, would he? Not after he went to all the trouble of savin' her!"

Mitch hung his head. He hadn't thought about that.

"You eat up," said Bibbo. "Then we're gonna call her. Tell her you're okay. And soon as this storm lets up, I'm puttin' you on a plane back to her!"

"But . . . I can't take your money," Mitch stammered. In his moth-eaten hat and scratched-up leather jacket, Bibbo looked as broke as Mitch was. "It just wouldn't be right."

Bibbo laughed. "I'm richer than I look, kid! Hey, Jimmy, why don't you tell Mitch here how I became a millionaire?"

Jimmy told the story of how Bibbo won the lottery, and soon Mitch was laughing. It was funny, he thought, how much better he felt now. Jimmy and Bibbo were Superman's friends, and they didn't blame him for Superman's death. Nor did they dump on him for thinking badly of Superman earlier. He was lucky. He just wished Superman could know how he felt.

Several days later, as weak rays filtered through the clearing Metropolis sky, Lois Lane stood beside Martha and Jonathan Kent as they laid a bouquet of red roses among the other flowers piled before Superman's tomb.

Looks like people've come from all over to pay

tribute to him, Martha thought as she reached out to take Jonathan's hand.

Jonathan stared up at the memorial statue through glistening tears. "It doesn't bring him back to us, but it's something, seeing how folks loved him!"

Later that afternoon, Jimmy and Mitch walked through Centennial Park.

"I leave for the airport pretty soon," said Mitch. "I . . . I want to thank you for all you've done—you and Bibbo. I just wish I could tell Superman's family how sorry I am . . . for everything."

"I know how you feel," said Jimmy. "So I thought maybe you'd like to come here!"

Mitch stared, awestruck, at the caped statue atop the imposing granite monument above Superman's tomb.

"This is where Superman is buried! Anything you have to say, you can say to Superman himself," Jimmy said, stepping back to give the boy some privacy.

Mitch knelt before Superman's tomb. "Hi, Superman," he whispered. "I feel kinda stupid, talking to a statue, but who knows? My grandma says my dead grandpa can hear us, so maybe you can too. See, I used to figure you for a real loser." Mitch shook his head, disgusted. "Shows what a zero I was. I know better than that now. You laid it on the line for us! My old man had cut out, but not you! Thanks to you, my mom and baby sister are okay. When I get home, I'll try to get along better with Ma. It's the least I can do to pay you back. With Dad gone, I can see now, she really needs my help."

Mitch stepped back beside Jimmy. "Thanks for letting me stay with you while I was here. Thanks for everything," he said, shaking Jimmy's hand as they walked out of Centennial Park. "It was great, but for some reason I can't wait to get home."

He held out his hand, and a cab pulled up to the curb. "Metropolis Airport!" Mitch said as he hopped inside. Mitch decided that, when he got home, he was going to work hard and pay Bibbo and Jimmy back the money they'd given him. But he knew the kindness and respect they had shown him was worth more than he could ever repay. *They're good men and worthy to be Superman's friends,* Mitch thought. *I'd like to be like them when I grow up.*

At the airport, Jonathan and Martha hugged Lois good-bye as a long-haired boy wearing a backward baseball cap rushed past. "Wish I was as eager to get home as that lad," said Jonathan. "Well, time to get on board, I guess."

Lois hugged the Kents a final time. "Don't forget," Lois said, "if you ever need me, I'll be there for you!"

As she watched them go through the gate, Lois thought about how the Kents had found Clark as a baby and raised him as their own son. No child could have had more loving parents, she realized.

Martha seemed to be coming to terms with Clark's death, Lois thought as she turned away from the gate, but Lois was worried about Jonathan. It almost seemed as if he blamed himself for his son's death.

In the middle of the night, an alarm sounded in Lex Luthor's lush penthouse apartment.

Luthor sprang from his bed and ran into the living room, where he punched a control panel concealed in the wall. "Identify the problem," he said.

A computerized voice replied, "Infrared sensors registering movement in outsector ten."

Supergirl raced into the room, transforming her nightgown into her Supergirl costume as she ran. "I heard the alarm, Lex. What's wrong? Where is outsector ten?"

"Superman's tomb, love!" Luthor growled.

"What?" gasped Supergirl. "Can Superman be alive?"

"It's impossible," Lex said firmly. "But his body has definitely been moved. I'd like you to investigate."

"Right away!" said Supergirl. As she ran toward the windows, the glass slid back as if by magic. Then she took off into the air.

"Use the secret access tunnel," he called after her. "Hurry, love. I'll meet you there as soon as I can!" As Lex stared after her, he wondered, *Could Superman still be alive?*

Supergirl flew west to Metropolis's Centennial Park and soared past the memorial statue over Superman's tomb. Ignoring a derelict asleep on a nearby park bench, she landed beside a subway ventilator shaft protected by a heavy grill.

Behind a hollow rock she found the hidden panel that Luthor's security people had installed there. She flipped a switch, and the grill slid back with the whirr of well-oiled machinery.

Supergirl took a deep breath. *So far, so good,* she thought.

The man on the park bench sat up. He was a lookout, and from beneath his ragged coat he pulled out a portable cellular phone. With half-frozen hands he dialed a number.

"This is Rusty," he said. "Sorry to wake you,

Lieutenant Sawyer, but I think I may have seen a ghost!"

Supergirl crept through the ventilator shaft. A large mechanical hatchway opened smoothly. She peered around the door.

The coffin was empty. Superman's body was gone. And beyond the slab on which the coffin lay, a jagged hole was ripped in the wall of the crypt.

As Lex Luthor's limousine cruised to a stop near Superman's crypt, a police car pulled up behind it. Lieutenant Maggie Sawyer stepped out and slammed the door behind her. Luthor was surprised to see her there, but he stepped from his limousine to greet her.

As they walked toward the ventilator shaft, Luthor explained about the secret entrance to the tomb, originally created, he said, when it was supposed to house a time capsule, not Superman's body. Then he told her that Superman's body had been moved.

As they entered the ventilator shaft and walked through the hatchway, Maggie Sawyer pulled a flashlight from her pocket. The beam shone on Supergirl, standing beside the empty coffin. Superman's body was missing, but where had it gone? Maggie stared at the hole in the wall of the crypt in amazement. It appeared to lead deep into the Earth.

"It looks like someone *has* stolen Superman's body," Supergirl said, "since it looks like the tomb was broken *into*, not *out* of." She pointed at the hole. "It leads into a tunnel with two main branches. I've explored one branch. There seem to be creatures, humans and . . . others . . . living in it, but it leads to a dead end. I haven't explored the other branch yet."

"Then let's do it now," said Lex. Cautiously, he stepped through the jagged hole and into the tunnel.

In a complex far beneath the earth, the Guardian stalked down the secret corridors of Project Cadmus. From an open door, Dubbilex called out to him. "We have a problem," the horned telepath began. "Westfield is locked in Lab Seven with an advanced study team in violation of all known protocols. He's set psionic buffers around the lab so I can't probe it telepathically. Using the computer system, I've undermined the security locks. But I wanted you to be with me when I activated the overrides."

The Guardian and Dubbilex stopped before Lab Seven. Dubbilex punched a series of buttons on the access panel. There was a hiss as the doors slid open. Inside, Westfield and a team of technicians in white lab coats whirled, startled by the interruption. On an examination table in the center of the room lay Superman's body.

The Guardian grabbed Westfield by the collar and

forced him against a wall. "You have no authorization for this!" he growled angrily.

"The President said . . . let Metropolis hold the funeral. I interpreted that to mean that after the funeral, my original authorization to collect all alien bodies would resume!"

"What were you planning to do?" growled the Guardian. "Dissect him?"

"I . . . I plan to clone him," Westfield stammered. "To bring him back to life!" Westfield hurriedly explained that Superman's mind could be partially reconstructed using Dubbilex's psychic impressions of him, and that they could, in fact, create a being who was close to Superman.

The Guardian dropped Westfield. "I don't know," he sighed. "I think you all ought to have your heads examined, but maybe we do owe it to Superman—and the world—to try."

Westfield smiled, satisfied. "You'll see, Guardian. In time, the world will come to learn I'm right."

Dubbilex scowled. Westfield was convincing, but the telepath still wasn't sure that what Westfield proposed was ethical.

Supergirl, Lex Luthor, and Maggie Sawyer had been following the winding tunnel for miles when Maggie shone her flashlight at the dripping ceiling.

"We must be under the Hob's River by now," said Maggie. "We'd better go carefully."

Suddenly there was a deafening roar. Beyond them, the tunnel roof crumbled. River water poured through the gaping hole like a torrent.

As they were swept along on the roaring tide, Supergirl encased Maggie and Lex in an invisible protective energy shield. Bobbing atop the rushing current, safe now in their force field cocoon, Supergirl, Maggie Sawyer, and Lex Luthor were carried back toward the hole in Superman's underground crypt.

Thirty minutes later, the three explorers stumbled back into Superman's empty tomb. Lieutenant Sawyer was worried. "How can I tell the people of Metropolis that Superman's body has been stolen?" she wondered.

Lex Luthor agreed. "Before making any announcements, perhaps we should discuss this with the mayor. I'm certain he would agree that if this news leaked out, it could cause a riot."

Outside the tomb, Supergirl leapt into the air, leaving Lieutenant Sawyer and Luthor behind on the ground. As they returned to their cars, both Luthor and Maggie Sawyer wondered what had caused the explosion that had flooded the tunnels. What was it meant to cover up? And had Director Westfield been involved in the disaster?

• • •

The Underworlders heard it first. "A rumble like the sound of an old freight train," said Charlie, tilting his head to listen. Then they saw it—a wall of river water that frothed white and wicked as it reached for them. Then they felt it—an icy fist that swept them aside, smashing anything and anyone in its path.

Suddenly, the humans and nonhumans who made their homes in Underworld were scrambling for their lives.

Six

The Kents drove their pickup truck from the airport to their farm under gloomy skies.

Jonathan took their bags inside and headed into the barn. "Guess I better see to the milking," he said despondently.

Martha looked after him. Jonathan had been her strength during Clark's funeral. But now it seemed the fight had gone out of him. Martha was worried.

BZZZZZZZZZZZZZZZZ!

Lois woke with a start. She was in her apartment. It was five in the morning. *What was that noise?* she wondered. *The alarm? No. The phone!*

She snatched up the receiver and mumbled "Hello?" Then she came instantly awake. She listened intently to Perry White, her managing editor, on the other end. Then she sat up in amazement. "What do you mean Metropolis is flooding?"

Lois slammed down the phone and jumped out of bed. But as she slipped on her clothes, she wondered why she had agreed to cover the disaster. *What good would it do?* Although she knew she had to continue on bravely, it seemed to be getting harder for her, not easier. After all, all the reporting in the world hadn't saved Superman.

"Come on, Neep-Nose! Take my hand and I'll get you out of that mess!"

Charlie grabbed the tiny pink hand of the little creature and pulled him onto the abandoned subway platform where the Underworlders had taken refuge from the rising water.

From amid the flood, an aquatic telepath called Tele-Tusk squawked for Charlie's attention. In his flipperlike hands, the walrus creature held up a blasting cap that bore the distinctive logo of Project Cadmus. Images poured into Charlie's mind like a movie, telling him that Tele-Tusk had found the blasting cap near the hole that was flooding Underworld.

Somebody has caused this mess on purpose, Charlie realized. *And it doesn't take a brain surgeon to figure out who is the culprit!*

. . .

At the Metropolis Stock Exchange, Lois tried to interview disgruntled workers lugging reams of soggy paper up from the basement.

"One of the old subway tunnels probably gave out!" a thin man grumbled.

"I don't know," said a plump woman. "My cousin James—he's a sanitation worker—was picking up the trash near the river. Said it sounded like there was an explosion under Superman's grave!"

An explosion?! Lois rushed from the Stock Exchange to Centennial Park. There she forced her way past guards stationed nearby and stormed into Superman's tomb, only to find that it was empty. The coffin was gone. And there was a hole ripped in the side of the crypt. Whatever she'd been expecting, it wasn't this.

Behind her a voice demanded, "What are you doing here?"

Lois whirled. Maggie Sawyer stood behind her in full riot gear.

"What's going on, Maggie?" asked Lois. "Because one way or another I'm going to find out!"

Maggie had known all along the city couldn't keep the disappearance of Superman's body a secret. "All right, Lois," she said. "I'll tell you what I know."

Clearly and concisely, Maggie gave Lois the details of her adventure the night before.

• • •

Lois stood on the embankment overlooking Hob's River. Maggie, Supergirl, and Luthor had all discovered that Superman's body was missing, Lois thought sadly. But she, who loved him, was the last to know. "Whoever flooded the tunnels must have stolen Clark's body!" Lois said to herself.

"Miss Lane! Miss Lane! Down here!" a voice from the river called.

Lois recognized Charlie instantly. He was being carried along in the water in the mouth of another Underworld creature, Bubble-Up, who looked very much like a giant frog. Lois ran down the steps to the river's edge as Charlie climbed out of Bubble-Up's mouth and onto the landing.

"Did you Underworlders cause the flood?" Lois asked.

"Why would we want to destroy our own home?" Charlie answered. "But we know who *did* do it! What we can't figure out is *why* they did it!"

"Someone stole Superman's body through a hole burrowed into Underworld. They covered their tracks by flooding the tunnels," said Lois. "You say you know who caused the flood?"

Charlie held out the blasting cap marked with the Cadmus logo. "Someone at Project Cadmus did it. So Cadmus must have Superman's body."

Lois knew immediately what she had to do, and Charlie offered to help. Superman had aided Underworld more than once, he told Lois, and the Underworlders would be eager to return the favor. While Charlie assembled a small crew of Underworlders with useful powers, Lois hurried home to get her scuba gear.

Lois hoped that the Underworlders' powers would prove as helpful as Charlie thought, because they were going to attempt the impossible. They were going to invade Project Cadmus and steal back Superman's body.

Covered in a wet suit, Lois Lane slipped into the icy river. Beneath the surface were Charlie and Neep-Nose, who were being ferried inside Bubble-Up's pouch alongside the walruslike telepath Tele-Tusk. The four Underworlders, traveling beneath the water, escorted Lois through the hole where the river water ran into Underworld tunnels. They soon reached a large mechanical bulwark that kept the river water from flooding Cadmus.

Charlie had told Lois that little Neep-Nose could disrupt and displace the molecules in solid objects, but Lois was still amazed as the tiny Underworlder took her hand and dragged her, Charlie, and Tele-Tusk through the bulwark and into Project Cadmus, leaving Bubble-Up behind in the water.

A guard on the other side of the wall whirled,

surprised, as they appeared. As he drew his gun, Tele-Tusk tackled him, slamming the gun aside. Then Charlie swung his fist, knocking the guard out.

Lois removed her mask and flippers. The guard lay unconscious at her feet.

Tele-Tusk placed his fingertips on the guard's head and searched his mind for the whereabouts of Superman's body. Tele-Tusk received an image of Lab Seven.

"This way, Miss Lane," Charlie pointed.

They rushed through corridors and hid from Cadmus personnel for what seemed like hours, but soon Lab Seven was before them. Neep-Nose phased his hand through the access grid, and the door slid open. Swiftly they stepped inside, then gaped in horror.

Superman was lying on a slab. Wires taped to his body were connected to gleaming monitors. Lois was outraged. She ran over and tried to lift him. "Help me!" she said. "We have to take him back. This isn't right!"

Suddenly Tele-Tusk received an image. He grabbed Lois, Charlie, and Neep-Nose and pulled them from the lab and down a corridor. They had to keep hidden, Tele-Tusk explained telepathically. The Guardian and Dubbilex were rushing toward the lab.

. . .

The Guardian gazed at Superman's body while Dubbilex checked the readings on the monitors. "Superman has moved," Dubbilex stated.

"Or someone has moved him," murmured the Guardian. "But who?"

"Oddly enough, I have no idea," answered Dubbilex. "I suspect a powerful telepath has been at work here. We'd better sound the alarm!"

WEEoooWEEoooWEEooo!

The alarm shrieked as Lois donned her scuba mask. Neep-Nose grabbed her, then Charlie and Tele-Tusk, and dragged them undetected through the bulwark and into the water.

"We weren't able to get Superman out of here, but now that I know where he is, I won't give up," Lois said as they surfaced.

That night, Lois sat at her desk at the *Daily Planet*, typing up her story. Even with the blasting cap, she knew she had no proof that Cadmus was implicated in Superman's disappearance. If she accused them, Cadmus would deny everything. But that didn't matter to her. She wasn't able to save Clark's life, but she was determined to save his body from desecration. Maybe her reporting was good for something after all.

Beneath the azure sky, Jonathan Kent stood before the partially filled impact crater where Clark had arrived on Earth. In his hand he clutched a copy of the Smallville *Star*. The headline read SUPERMAN'S BODY MISSING.

"Jonathan David Kent, what are you doing way out here in the cold?" Martha scolded him as she hurried across the icy field. "You know what Lois said when she called. She told us Clark's body was missing. But she swears she'll get him back." Martha wrapped a coat around Jonathan's shoulders, but he didn't seem to notice.

"This is where the rocket brought him to Earth. He seemed so helpless then. I swore I'd protect him . . . I'd keep him safe. But I couldn't. I just—" Jonathan grabbed his chest and fell to his knees as his words faded. Then he toppled to the icy ground.

"Jonathan!" screamed Martha. She clutched her husband's unconscious body to her breast. "Oh, Jonathan! Not you too!"

Luthor's private gymnasium was like everything else at his corporate headquarters—equipped with the best. That included his trainer, a woman named Sasha Green, whom Luthor had hired to provide him with a top-drawer workout.

Though his body automatically went through the routine of thrust and parry, Luthor's mind wasn't on his karate. It was on Superman, and how their battles had lent savor to his life. But now there was no challenge, not since the Man of Steel had—

Suddenly Sasha kicked Luthor's feet out from under him. He landed hard on the mat. "Keep daydreaming like that, Mr. Luthor, and you're wasting your money," Sasha laughed.

Luthor looked up at her, growling. "Nobody does that to me! You have no idea what trouble you've—"

Just then Supergirl ran into the gym, followed by Lois Lane. "I know you hate to have your training sessions interrupted, Lex, but this is really important," she said.

"Hello, Lex," said Lois, offering the billionaire her hand as he climbed to his feet. "It's obvious you're not like your father. If that overweight old power broker had ever been drop-kicked like that, he'd have the kicker put on ice!"

"How very true," Lex murmured, shooting Sasha an enigmatic glance as he walked from the gym beside Lois and Supergirl. "And now, Miss Lane, what brings you here?"

"I want you to read a column I wrote before it goes to press," said Lois, handing Lex a stack of papers.

Luthor scanned the article. "You mean it was *Project Cadmus* who stole Superman's body—in order to *clone* it? Why, this is an outrage!"

"I'm afraid when I publish the article, they'll just deny it and move his body somewhere else," Lois explained. "Then we'll never get it back."

Lex assured her that, now that they knew for certain where Superman's body was, Supergirl would retrieve it.

"Thank you, Lex," Lois said. "I knew you'd understand. That's why I came to you." Leaving his office, she heaved a sigh of relief.

"Code blue! Code blue! This man is in cardiac arrest!" called an attendant as he pulled Jonathan Kent from the ambulance and rushed him through the emergency room of Kansas's Lowell County General Hospital. "Get him into emergency!"

Martha climbed from the ambulance and hurried behind them. "It must be the stress caused by Clark's death," she explained. "Jonathan hasn't been himself for days!"

As she waited for the doctors, Martha thought to herself, *I just hope he pulls through. With my son gone, I just can't bear the thought of losing Jonathan too.*

Supergirl kissed Luthor for luck and soared through the window of his penthouse suite. Lex had shown her a copy of Cadmus's layout. *Much of Project Cadmus has been disrupted by the flood,* she thought. *"I should have little trouble finding and retrieving Superman's body."*

Lex Luthor watched as Supergirl left. It was now time to turn his attention to other matters.

In the women's locker room, Sasha Green showered and dressed hurriedly. She was meeting her friends after work and she couldn't wait to tell them how she had bested Mr. Luthor in their workout. Suddenly a voice called her name.

Sasha whirled, surprised. "What are you doing here? This is the women's locker."

"That's of little concern to me," said Luthor as he reached for her.

Sasha had time for only a muffled scream before she lost consciousness.

Supergirl entered Project Cadmus undetected, but her presence did not remain secret for long. Troops rushed to stop her, but she attacked them with psionic blasts. Zipping through the tunnels and corridors, she felled anyone who challenged her.

In Lab Seven, she stood before Superman's body. Overcome by the sadness of his death, she blinked back tears. Then she carefully lifted Superman into her arms and flew from the lab. Now she would return him to his final resting place.

• • •

It was night. Lois Lane and Lex Luthor were waiting in Centennial Park as Supergirl landed before them. All was ready, said Luthor.

As Supergirl replaced Superman's body in his coffin, Lois thought about how she had been engaged to Clark. She would soon have made vows to love and honor him for the rest of her life.

Reaching out to touch his face, she whispered, "I do." In her mind he slipped the ring on her finger. In her heart, she kissed him. And they lived happily ever after.

"If you two wouldn't mind," Luthor said, interrupting Lois's thoughts, "I'd like to be alone for a few minutes."

Lois and Supergirl left the crypt together. His eyes glittering, Luthor whirled on the coffin. "Gotcha! I knew I'd bury you one day," he snarled. "There isn't a man on Earth who can stop me now from doing whatever I please. That's the reason I killed Sasha— just to prove to you that I was king again. When they find her body, evidence will point toward the janitor. And you can't do a blessed thing about it. You're dead! You are nothing! And I am back on top! Once again, Superman, Metropolis is mine!"

Luthor stared down at the coffin for a moment

longer. Then, smiling grimly, he strode from the tomb and into the evening air.

"His heart has stopped again!" the doctor groaned, pounding on Jonathan's chest. "He's not fighting at all!"

Martha clutched her husband's hand. "Jonathan," she sobbed, "don't leave me here all alone!"

As Jonathan slipped further from consciousness, a figure appeared before him. It was Clark—or was it just a dream?

"It's me, Pa," Clark said. "Don't be afraid."

Jonathan reached out and clasped his boy's hand. "I'm coming, son," he said.

"Doctor, he's flat-lined," cried the nurse. "We're losing him!"

Seven

Somewhere between this world and the beyond, a bright light was shining. Jonathan knew if his son entered the light, he'd never see him again.

Suddenly, Jor-El, Clark's Kryptonian father, appeared beside them. Turning to Jonathan, he said, "You cannot cross over. It is not your time!" Jor-El turned to Clark. "Come, Kal-El!" he said, calling his son by his Kryptonian name.

As if in a trance, Clark started to follow his Kryptonian father. In a panic, Jonathan clutched at his boy's shirt, which tore away, revealing the Superman costume beneath it. Ignoring Jonathan's interference, Jor-El took Clark's arm and led him through the mist and into the light.

"Jonathan Kent, you listen to me!" cried Martha. "Don't you give up! You're too blamed stubborn to just give up!"

As the doctor pounded Jonathan's chest, Lois Lane burst into the emergency room. "I got the first flight out!" she cried. "Martha, how is he?"

"He'd been warned about his heart, but he wouldn't slow down!" Martha said with a catch in her voice. "Especially these last few weeks. I wonder whether he brought this on himself, to try to get closer to Clark. He loved that boy as much as life itself!"

Lois put her arm around Martha as they stared down at Jonathan. *He's as pale as death,* Lois thought. If love for Clark was drawing him away, then maybe their love might keep him here. Lois prayed their love would be enough.

Jonathan reached for the fading figures of Clark and Jor-El but lost them in the swirling mist. Looking around, Jonathan suddenly found himself in Korea, dressed in jungle fatigues. His mission—to rescue a captured airman.

Bathed in the harsh light of the heavens, Jonathan raised his head and sniffed. Something was burning. Cautiously, he stalked through the underbrush. Ahead of him, in a clearing, a farmhouse was on fire. Beside it lay a fallen farmer.

Gently, Jonathan turned the farmer over and looked down into his face. To his amazement, the dying farmer was his own brother.

"Harry!" Jonathan cried, lifting his brother into his arms. "What are you doing in Korea?"

"This ain't Korea," Harry said flatly. "Don't you remember? I fell under the thresher machine back on Pa's farm. I'm dead, Jonny. We're all dead here. But you don't belong here. Neither does Clark. Go get your boy, Jonny."

Harry fell limply in Jonathan's arms. When Jonathan looked up, he found himself in a cornfield.

Looks a lot like Dad's old field back in Kansas, he thought as he stepped forward eagerly. Suddenly the ground gave way, and Jonathan was falling through rotten planks into an old abandoned well, just as he had back when he was a child. Only this time, he tumbled through the bottom of the well and out into space.

As Jonathan fell, swirling clouds enveloped him. Then, with a thump, he landed softly on a grassy knoll. Beyond him, pastel spires soared upward.

It's the world of Krypton! Just like I visualized it from Clark's stories! thought Jonathan. Looking down the hill, he noticed a funeral procession. Then he gaped in alarm. There was Clark, being carried on a litter by several Kryptonians.

Jonathan ran down the hill. "Son!" he shouted. "Look around you! You've got to wake up!"

Shrouded wraiths grabbed Jonathan and dragged him back, but he kept shouting, calling out to his son. Clark opened his eyes. Around him he saw Kryptonian spirits—or were they demons?

Jonathan struggled and broke free of the wraiths that held him. And at his touch they turned to dust. "Come, son. Now let's get away from here."

"I can't deny death," Clark said flatly. "But I can take you away from this." He lifted his father and together they flew into the air.

In the distance, the Tunnel of Life swirled. *It's like looking into the turbulent black eye of a tornado*, Jonathan thought.

"Listen to me, son!" Jonathan cried. "I'm convinced that the only reason you're here is that Clark Kent was raised with the human concept of mortality. But maybe Kal-El doesn't have to die. For once I'm begging you not to think like an Earthling!"

Clark looked at his father. Pa had always had such faith in him, such love. Clark couldn't bear to disappoint him. "I'll try, Pa," he said. "For you, I'll try!"

Clark wrapped his arms around his father, and together they flew into the Tunnel of Life.

"We've given Jonathan as much stimulant as is safe, Martha," said the doctor. "I hope—"

"I made it," Jonathan murmured. Martha and Lois looked down—Jonathan had regained consciousness. "We *both* made it! I brought Clark back to us!"

Jonathan smiled at them, a smile filled with love. Then he closed his eyes and drifted off to sleep. It was like a miracle, the doctor said. Jonathan's heart was beating strongly now. With tears in their eyes, Lois and Martha hugged each other. They would monitor his recovery, but they knew that Jonathan was going to be okay.

Eight

Superboy . . .

OOOT! OOOT! OOOT! OOOT!

The alarms at Project Cadmus blared. Cadmus troops rushed down the hall, weapons at the ready, with the Guardian at their head. "We've got a Code Red in Lab Thirteen," the Guardian shouted. "A power surge caused an explosion."

A trooper tried the lab door. "It's jammed shut, sir!" he said.

Director Westfield rushed up. "Make sure nothing happens to the experiment in there!" he shouted.

At the Guardian's order, a trooper raised a bazookalike weapon and blew open the door. Inside, the lab was a smoldering shambles. Liquid poured from a large, shattered glass tube, and wires hung limply inside it.

"No," Westfield whispered. "He wasn't ready!"

"Help!" cried a voice from above. "Get me down!"

Looking up, they noticed a scientist hanging from the ceiling, pinned there by pipes twisted in a neat bow.

"Dr. Packard," Westfield demanded, "what happened?"

"Experiment Thirteen started to fight off the input and broke free. He ripped apart these pipes, tied me here, then disappeared into the air duct! The code words . . . the instructions . . . were never implanted! We have absolutely no control over him!"

On the other side of the Cadmus facility, near the Lookout, a favorite hangout for local teens, the protective grating of an air shaft burst off its hinges with a loud *KLANG!* Several kids leaned out of cars to see what had caused the racket.

Apparently from nowhere, a dark-haired teenager leapt into the air before them. He was wearing skin-tight spandex with an S-shield on his chest and a leather jacket.

The local kids gawked. "Look, it's Superman! No! It looks more like Superboy—"

"Hey!" the teenager snapped angrily, hovering

above them. "Don't *ever* call me Superboy!" Then he soared off into the night air.

The Man of Steel . . .

Beneath a half-destroyed skyscraper, a street gang called the Sharks faced off against another gang called the Dragons. A battle was about to begin for control of the neighborhood's drug trade.

"Look at what the Sharks're packin'," muttered a Dragon called Hype, hefting his AK–47.

Suddenly a shell ripped through Hype, blowing him almost in half.

"Sharks ain't got guns! They got ordnance!" screamed another Dragon as he opened fire. A moment later, he too fell lifeless to the ground.

Bullets the size of rockets smashed into the rubble of the skyscraper, hitting the girders with the ominous sound of doom!

To the repeated explosions, Henry Johnson started to awaken. For days he had been buried beneath the rubble of the fallen skyscraper. Miraculously he had now awakened. He reached up, and with all his might managed to shove aside a girder.

Suddenly the air was split by the scream of approaching squad cars.

The Sharks dashed for their cars, hooting with joy over the power of their new superweapons. Not far behind them, the squad cars screeched to a halt.

"It's the skyscraper that Doomsday monster knocked down. Looks like a war zone there!" one of the cops said as he leapt from the car.

His partner grabbed his arm and hauled him back. "Wait! Something's coming up out of the rubble!"

Henry Johnson shoved aside the final girder. His ebony skin was cut, and his overalls were torn. Lit by the police car's headlights, Johnson looked like a man risen from the grave.

Turning toward the policemen, with a voice like thunder, he rumbled, "Doomsday! Where's Doomsday? I've gotta stop Doomsday!"

The Cyborg . . .

A young couple and their son, Jake, wandered the streets of Metropolis, looking up at the tall buildings, then down again at their tour map.

"Where next?" asked the boy.

"The *Daily Planet*," said Jake's father. "There's a plaque over there where Superman died."

"The *Planet's* got a globe on top," said Jake, craning his neck up. "Hey, there it is! And there's the plaque!" he added, running over and pointing. "See? It's set in the sidewalk!"

" 'In memory of Superman. Killed on this spot while defending Metropolis,' " Jake's mother read aloud.

They stood there a moment silently. Then Jake glanced up. "Look!" he yelled. "Up in the sky!"

Soaring between the buildings was a caped figure, silhouetted against the bright city lights. The figure dipped low and landed before them. He was dressed in Superman's costume. The right half of his face, and the left half of his body, looked like Superman's. But the other half was robotic.

He's a Cyborg now, thought Jake. *Just like Darth Vader.*

The Cyborg yanked the plaque from the sidewalk. As he looked at it, his eyes began to glow red. The plaque smoked. Then, in a burst of heat, it was gone. The figure turned away.

"Wait," cried the father. "Why did you burn that plaque? Are . . . are you—?"

"Yes," the Cyborg said, leaping into the air. "I'm back!"

The Last Son of Krypton . . .

Beyond the Ellsworth Mountains in Antarctica, buried beneath the ice, was a technological fortress like no other on Earth. It was called the Fortress of Solitude and was the legacy of Superman's Kryptonian forefathers. It was created as a subsurface fortress by a two-hundred-millennia-old Kryptonian device called the Eradicator that had found its way to Earth. The device had eventually taken humanoid form and tried to transform Earth into a new Krypton, but Superman had destroyed the device and trapped the Eradicator where it could do no more harm.

Inside the Fortress, robot drones scurried around a bank of controls, making minute adjustments. Suddenly, within a clouded sphere, a mass of energy in human form appeared.

"Where am I?" the being asked. He moved through the sphere and looked around. "This is my Fortress. How did I get here?"

Reaching for one of the robot drones, he found that his hand passed through it. "I . . . I'm immaterial," the being exclaimed. "Just energy. What has happened to me?"

A screen flashed on before him, showing Superman's fight with Doomsday, Superman's death, and his burial.

"Dead," the being murmured. "No! It can't end this way! The body! The real power must be in the body. I must go to the tomb."

He crashed through the dome of the Fortress and soared into the air.

In an instant he was in Metropolis, within Superman's tomb. *The body is here,* thought the being. *Like a solar battery, it has absorbed and metabolized the energy of the sun for over thirty years.* The being reached through the lid of the coffin. *I can feel the raw power stirring within.*

At the being's touch, the body of Superman began to glow. As the light faded, the shadowy figure lifted Superman's cape and wrapped it around his shoulders. Sensing the surveillance cameras within the tomb, he passed his hand through their wiring, short-circuiting them.

As he staggered from the tomb, the being thought, *The light, so bright! Something has changed within me. I must return to the Fortress.*

Once inside the Fortress, he stood before an egg-shaped matrix that crackled with energy. "Bless Krypton and the House of El!" he cried. "Their legacy, the technology of this Fortress, has given me new life. This glorious Regeneration Matrix has insured that the heart of Krypton's Last Son keeps beating! It channels life-giving energies into me, now that I can no longer absorb them directly from the sun."

The being stepped away, deep in thought. *Once I could stare into the sun, see to the ends of the Earth. But now the dimmest light blinds me. If not for this visor, I would be helpless. But I am still strong! I still possess powers and abilities far beyond those of mortal men. I can still fly free of gravity's hold.* He stretched out his hand, and electrical power shot from his fingertips. *And I have been given* other *powers,* he thought grimly.

On the monitor overhead, the world news came on, interrupting the being's thoughts. There was trouble everywhere, but especially in Metropolis.

As he rose through the ceiling, the being knew now what he had to do. *I cannot rest while the world is in such a desperate state. The people cry out for me . . . for Superman. And the Last Son of Krypton must be their champion once more! I am needed in Metropolis.*

. . .

The jet soared over cities and fields, but Lois Lane didn't notice. She was lost in thought. Jonathan was getting better, but he kept insisting that Clark was alive. She wanted to believe him, desperately, but she knew Clark had died in her arms.

"Look!" screeched a child in the seat behind her. "Look! A flying man!"

Lois gazed out the window. Past the plane flew a red blur. *Could it be possible?* She couldn't fool herself. Couldn't let herself believe. That way lay madness.

But as she disembarked from the airplane in Metropolis, TV sets and radios blared word of multiple sightings and proclaimed the return of Superman.

If Clark has mysteriously returned from death, then his body must be missing! There is only one way to find out. Racing through a rain shower, she drove in rush-hour traffic toward Superman's tomb.

Nine

Lois was in the midst of gridlocked traffic in a driving rain when her police scanner came on.

"Superman's body is missing again," the police radios squawked.

So it's true! His body is *gone! Clark's back!* Lois thought with growing excitement. *But . . . how can it be true?* she asked herself. Then she remembered Director Westfield. *I wonder if Westfield has stolen his body again.*

She got off at the next exit and headed for Project Cadmus.

At Project Cadmus, the Cyborg entered, as ground troops, under the Guardian's command, bombarded him with energy waves from shock cannons. Unhurt, the Cyborg stopped before the Guardian and demanded, "I've come for Doomsday."

"S-superman?" the Guardian stammered. "I watched you die with my own eyes."

"I've come back," said the Cyborg. "I'm different, because of the damage I've suffered. But it is me. I am Superman."

"Whoever you are, Doomsday's dead," said the Guardian. "His body is contained in the finest security vault on Earth."

"Who knows what constitutes death . . . or life . . . for Doomsday?" the Cyborg said. "I'm getting him off the Earth while I have the chance."

Using his X-ray vision, the Cyborg spotted Doomsday's body on a level far below. He spun at superspeed, drilling through the floors, until he arrived at the maximum security cell where Doomsday's body rested.

Metal wires and probes snaked from the Cyborg's robot hand to interface with the computer. He overrode the security system and commanded the vault to open.

Inside the vault, Doomsday was bound with heavy cables fashioned of the strongest metals on Earth. The cables were attached to monitors so that if Doomsday so much as twitched, Cadmus authorities would know it immediately.

Swiftly, the Cyborg ripped Doomsday free. Thick cables dangled from Doomsday's limp body as the Cyborg lifted him and flew up and away.

. . .

Meanwhile, Lois pulled her car off the road and climbed out into the rain. Project Cadmus was below her. She'd have to think of a way to get inside. Suddenly someone—was it really Superman?—roared overhead. Soon he was lost in the turbulent clouds.

The Cyborg carried Doomsday to an asteroid, beyond the orbit of Mars. He bound the creature to the rock with cables and attached a warning device. *If anyone tampers with these bonds, I'll know,* he thought. Then he hurled the asteroid off into the infinite void of deep space.

Lois squinted into the driving rain, searching the sky for Superman's return.

"You are Lois Lane, the one who first named me Superman," said a voice behind her.

Startled, Lois turned and looked into the Cyborg's glistening metal face.

"I know I'm different, perhaps unpleasant to look at. But it's me!"

Lois didn't quite believe him. "How could you come back? You're part—machine?"

The Cyborg couldn't remember how he came to be this way, he told her. Because of the beating he'd received at Doomsday's hands, there was much he didn't remember. "But I do remember a farm . . . in Kansas," he said. "And the name Kent. It's frustrating. I've been through so much. I'm still not . . . the way I should be."

"Prove who you are," said Lois. "Come with me!"

In Professor Hamilton's laboratory, the Cyborg stood inside a giant sphere.

"I've run more scans on Superman than anyone on Earth," Professor Hamilton assured her. "If this man is a fraud, I'll know it!"

He punched a button, and the Cyborg was surrounded by a nimbus of energy.

"This man's machine half is made of Kryptonian metals. As for his biological half, all the DNA matches up with Superman's," the professor murmured. "Very probably, this *is* Superman returned to life!"

Suicide Slum was a rotten place to stop for a red light, so the driver tensed when a burly bum staggered toward his car, then pulled a pistol from his pocket. "Outta the car! Move it!" the bum growled.

Suddenly a caped and visored man landed between the carjacker and his victim. The carjacker's bullets bounced off the shield on the man's chest. "You can't be Superman! He's dead!" he exclaimed as he turned to run.

"Running is futile," said the visored man. Light-ning cracked from his hands, engulfing the carjacker, who fell to the ground. "You cannot escape the power of the Last Son of Krypton."

"Burns. Can't . . . be Superman. He busts peo-ple . . . not toasts 'em," the carjacker moaned.

"How little you know," said the Kryptonian. "I have passed through the fire and the darkness and have been changed! I have risen from the dead to continue the never-ending battle. I shall use the power that is mine as Krypton's Last Son to bring justice to this Earth. And all who sin shall know the wrath of Superman!"

Henry Johnson heard gunfire and dashed from the YMCA, where he'd been working out. A child, caught in the cross fire in a turf war between two rival gangs, lay in the gutter. It looked as if the boy had been hit by a small missile. *Oh no,* he thought. *Please, it can't be possible!*

A black Mercedes was screeching away. Without a second thought, Henry Johnson took a shortcut across an empty lot, jumped over a junked car, and leapt onto the passenger side of the Mercedes as it roared past. He wrenched the powerful weapon from the gunman's hand.

"Scrape 'im off, Dutch!" yelled the gunman.

Dutch swerved the car, and Henry was crushed between the car door and an alley wall.

Toastmasters . . . secret weapons. I destroyed the prototypes. What're they doing . . . in Metropolis? thought Henry as he slid down the wall and into unconsciousness.

Several days later, Henry Johnson, wrapped in bandages, sat in his private workshop in the basement of his apartment building, constructing a high-tech suit of armor.

It's my fault that kid is dead, Henry thought as he polished a giant, long-handled hammer. *I designed those weapons. How can I make a thing like that right? Superman saved my life once. He said make it count for something. I owe him that much. Now Metropolis needs a Superman. It's time to put this design to the test!*

Henry lifted an armored chest plate. On it was bolted a shimmering copy of Superman's shield. Quietly, he began to strap it on.

Dutch peered through the grimy basement window. He couldn't tell what Henry Johnson was doing, but it didn't matter. He'd soon be dead. *That will teach him to mess with the Sharks,* Dutch thought. Smashing the window, he hurled a bomb, which hit the furnace and exploded. Suddenly the basement was in flames.

Henry heard screams from the apartments overhead. Pulling on the armor's mask, he ignited the thrusters in his boots and rocketed through the wall of flame up to the first floor. "Get back," he rumbled, smashing through the apartment door with his massive hammer. "The Man of Steel is coming through!"

By the time the fire engines had arrived, he had everyone out of the brownstone.

Lois Lane raced up to the building as the Man of Steel was rocketing away. *Darn!* she thought. *I missed him. But whoever he is, he's doing Superman's work—saving the lives of others at great risk to his own.*

At the *Daily Planet,* Lois Lane stood by the copy machine, confused and annoyed. "How many Supermen are there now?" she asked Jimmy Olsen. "Three . . . four?"

"Lois, Lois, Lois," came a voice from behind her. "I thought we had a deal. You know—I save the world, you write it up, we both end up on page one."

Lois whirled. Sitting at her chair with his feet on her desk was a teenager in a skintight suit and leather jacket.

"But no," the teenager rambled on. "I save a

jogger from some joyriding punks and all I get is page six. No byline even. Y'know, I would've gotten rid of Doomsday too! I was gettin' around to it!"

"You can't be . . . Superman," Lois said.

Jimmy glanced at the S-shield on the teenager's chest. "More like Super*boy*," he muttered.

The teenager grabbed Jimmy by the collar and held him upside down. "Listen, pal, don't call me Super*boy*!" he said between clenched teeth.

"S-sure. No problem . . . Superman?" Jimmy gasped, and the teenager dropped him to the ground.

"See, he's convinced," the teenager assured Lois.

"Look," she said, with half a smile. "The real Superman was old enough to shave."

"Okay, okay!" said the teenager. "You forced me to do this! It's supposed to be a secret, but, well . . . I'm—"

Superboy stopped midsentence and stared as a beautiful African-Asian girl left the newsroom. "Excuse me," he mumbled as he zoomed off after her.

As the girl walked from the building, the teenager scooped her high into the air.

"Put me down," she shrieked.

"You're way too hot to be a *newspaper* reporter," said the teenager.

"I'm Tana Moon. And you're one of the Supermen," she said, startled. "But you're so young!"

"Okay, okay! I'll tell you the secret. You see, I'm a clone of Superman!" said the teenager. "WGBS TV has been wild to have an exclusive with me. So far I haven't been so sure . . . but if a beautiful woman like you were covering my exploits, I just might consider signing with them. What do you say we talk about it?"

Tana smiled. She'd met men like him before, totally dazzled by a pretty face. He was bold, too, but something told her that, beneath his brash exterior, he was really a nice guy. "Okay!" she said with a grin. "Let's try WGBS!"

In Metropolis, the Man of Steel scoured the streets, searching for the child's murderers. He found them in a tenement apartment where an illegal drug trade was in progress.

He rocketed toward the building, smashing through a grimy window. One by one, he took out the dealers. Finally he grabbed their leader. "Where'd you get the guns, Dutch?" he rumbled.

"The T-toastmasters? The W-white R-rabbit—" Dutch stammered. Before he could say more, a shot through the shattered window stopped his heart.

On a nearby rooftop, a woman stepped into the shadows. She was an albino with white hair and skin. Her pink eyes assessed her work coldly.

"You had a bead on the Man of Steel, Rabbit?

Why'd you pop Dutch?" her lieutenant asked nervously.

"Dutch was singing his heart out," their leader said. "And if there's one thing I hate, it's a pigeon. Besides, I recognized that Man of Steel's voice. His *real* name is John Henry Irons, and he's potentially very profitable—if he'll join us. There's no point in killing him . . . yet."

Lex Luthor paced before his TV monitor–filled office wall. He was furious. The local station had announced that Superman's tomb was empty once again. Not even his own TV station, WLEX, had that scoop.

Why do I have to learn this news secondhand from the television like everyone else? Luthor wondered. The videocams and equipment that he positioned in the vault were top of the line. *How could their wires just fuse together?*

A second monitor featured the Man of Steel and his one-man war against the drug lords' new superweapons. A third offered an interview with the teenager who claimed to be Superman's clone.

Luthor punched the intercom. "Dr. Happersen," he growled to his assistant. "Get Packard at Cadmus here! And find out about the superweapons. I want to know who's selling them!"

. . .

The wing of a small plane clipped a building and spiraled toward the ground. "Help!" cried a voice into the radio.

Suddenly the plane lurched and leveled off. Beneath its fuselage, the visored Kryptonian held it steady as he gently brought it down in Riverside Park.

Nearby, Lois jumped from a cab. "Hold it right there! We need to talk," she said.

The Kryptonian lifted Lois in his arms and carried her to a nearby rooftop. "Who are you?" she asked. "What's your game?"

"I'm Superman, the Last Son of Krypton," he said. "There is no game."

"If you're really Superman, then tell me who I am," Lois murmured.

"You are Lois Lane, the reporter. Before my passing, you were an important part of my life."

His voice is softening, Lois thought excitedly. *He's beginning to sound like Clark.* "If you're Superman, tell me something only Superman could know," she said.

"I know . . . we were more than friends. You were engaged to Clark Kent," he said. "He loved and trusted you, even with his secret identity."

"Then you are—" Lois hesitated, unable to continue.

"I am . . . sorry. I grieve for your loss. But Kent is gone," he said. "There is only Superman now."

And with that, he took off into the sky and flew away.

Lois looked after the Kryptonian with tears in her eyes. If he was lying, someone had learned that Clark Kent was Superman. But if he was telling the truth, she'd lost Clark all over again.

Ten

Superboy was working unofficially with WGBS-TV now. No contracts had been signed yet, but all Metropolis knew that the beautiful new reporter, Tana Moon, covered his stories for WGBS exclusively.

WGBS had been tipped off that the infamous Iron Hand Gang was holed up in the Suicide Slum section of Hob's Bay. The gangsters were well armed and dangerous. Superboy decided that it was his duty as a hero to take them out.

Tana Moon and the WGBS news choppers followed Superboy's progress as he reached the villains' hideout and punched his way through the wall.

"Iron Hand, glass jaw!" he quipped as he single-handedly knocked the villains out.

After the fight, Superboy was, of course, interviewed by Tana Moon.

• • •

"Fine job, Tana. Our ratings are way up. Soon our Superman will be the only Superman," said Tana's boss, Vinnie Edge. "But next time, Superboy should fight someone with powers . . . and a costume."

"Sure, Vinnie," Tana joked. "You just tell me when, and I'll get it all on tape."

The superpowered teenager's exploits have already meant a viewer increase for WGBS, Vinnie thought. A larger, more impressive fight would mean even more viewers and more advertising revenue. Vinnie grinned evilly. "That can be arranged!"

The interior of the Metropolis Mercantile Bank was dark, save for a single tiny spotlight shining from the forehead of a burglar who hummed softly as he cracked the massive safe.

Suddenly he was snatched into the air by the visored Kryptonian. "You wouldn't kill me just for robbing a safe," the burglar stammered.

"Your crimes have hurt many people," said the Kryptonian. "I will make certain that you don't try this again!"

He then took the burglar's hands in his own and squeezed.

At Metropolis General Hospital, the doctor whispered to Lois Lane, "Never seen anything like it. Every bone in his hands was broken. He claims Superman did it."

"Could I ask your patient some questions?" Lois asked.

"You can try," said the doctor.

"This Superman who attacked you . . . what did he look like?" Lois asked the burglar.

"Sunglasses," the burglar moaned. "He wore sunglasses . . . like one big visor."

Lois sighed as she left the hospital room. *The visored Kryptonian knew about Clark. But he couldn't really be him. Clark wasn't cold or cruel. None of the Supermen was Clark . . . or?*

The Last Son of Krypton returned to the Fortress of Solitude in Antarctica, exhilarated by the work he had done. Robot drones hurried to lift off his cape as he looked around, pleased. Then he frowned.

"What is this?" he growled. Massive screens featured the news of Earth in which a teenager, a cyborg, and an armored man each wore the S-shield and claimed to be Superman.

As he stepped before the giant egg-shaped Regeneration Matrix, the Kryptonian ordered the computer to monitor and compile data on these pretenders. Then he reached out his hand, as if to absorb the Matrix's swirling energies.

• • •

Lex Luthor had brooded for days on the existence of the four new Supermen. *Who are they really?* he wondered, determined to get to the bottom of the mystery. He had not been able to control the original Superman. The influence of that super-hero had eclipsed Luthor's own power in Metropolis. But Luthor thought that, almost certainly, he could control at least one of the pretenders. And when he did, their power and prestige would enhance, not eclipse, his own.

He called his assistant, Dr. Happersen, into his office. "What have you learned about the new super-weapons the Man of Steel is trying to eradicate?" Luthor asked.

"The guns are called Toastmasters," said Dr. Happersen. "They're supplied by a woman called the White Rabbit."

A woman, thought Luthor. *Interesting.* Perhaps she would be his key to controlling the Man of Steel.

A pack of Sharks toting Toastmasters stalked the Man of Steel through Suicide Slum, as a gang member with a video camera taped their progress.

But Henry Johnson, the Man of Steel, was also stalking them. He dived at the Sharks from a rooftop, took out the gang, then grabbed the gang leader. "Where can I find the White Rabbit?" he rumbled.

"The . . . the Spi—!" The rest of the gang leader's words were drowned in a rattle of gunfire. The cameraman had shot him.

Before the cameraman could fire again, the Man of Steel pinned him to a wall. "Where's the Rabbit?" he growled.

"Not telling. Rather take my chances with you!" the cameraman snarled.

"You'll take your chances with the cops," said the Man of Steel as he lifted the camera. "The evidence against you is on this videotape!"

Lex Luthor's people paid a fortune to acquire a copy of that videotape. The sound enhancers working on the film had analyzed it. They thought the leader was about to say that the White Rabbit was staying at the "Spire" . . . the Metrospire Hotel.

If all goes according to plan, the Man of Steel will work for me, thought Luthor. *He'll be my star Superman on WLEX, and the world will know that I control him, as I control Supergirl. His prowess will enhance my own power.*

Luthor was feeling very pleased. It was time he had a Superman in his pocket.

• • •

The next day, Lois Lane rode in a chopper, covering another firefight between the Sharks and the Man of Steel on a pier far below.

"Hey, look who's there," said her pilot.

Superboy flew by, waving to Lois. "I know I ditched you and the *Planet* for Tana Moon and WGBS, but no hard feelings, right? Now watch me bail out the Man of Steel!"

He flew at the Sharks, deliberately drawing their fire. "Hey! What are those guys shooting?" he said to himself as he dodged the blasts. "Rockets?"

As Superboy dived into the fight, he didn't see gunfire from a Toastmaster rip through Lois Lane's chopper, kill the pilot instantly, then smash through the top of the cab into the rotary engine.

Lois leapt from the chopper seconds before it blew and plummeted toward the ground. The Man of Steel zoomed into the sky and, at the last second, caught her.

"The other Supermen have been tripping over themselves trying to convince the world they're the real thing! What about you?" she asked.

"I never said I was Superman!" he said. He put Lois down, then rocketed away.

• • •

Superboy was giving another interview with Tana Moon when the Man of Steel flew overhead and angrily jerked him into the sky.

"Most of the Sharks escaped," the Man of Steel said, "no thanks to you. What's worse, you didn't worry about who was behind you when you drew their fire. Now Miss Lane's pilot is dead."

At first, Superboy was horrified. He hadn't even thought about Lois's chopper. Then he got mad. "You're not Superman! I am! At least, I'm his clone! What right do you have to lecture me?"

The Man of Steel zoomed away without a word, leaving Superboy to try to convince himself that it wasn't his fault a man had died.

As he flew past the LexCorp Building, the Man of Steel was summoned by a Team Luthor trooper, a soldier in Lex Luthor's private army. "Mr. Luthor wants to see you. He has information on the White Rabbit. Follow me."

The Man of Steel landed on the LexCorp Building roof where Luthor was waiting in the shadows. He stepped forward, offering the Man of Steel a place as WLEX's star Superman. He would make him rich, he promised. And famous, with better coverage than WGBS gave Superboy. But the Man of Steel wasn't interested. He interrupted Luthor's speech with a demand. "Your goon said you had information on the Rabbit! What is it?"

"Check the Metrospire Hotel penthouse," Luthor said, slapping him on the back. "Get the Rabbit, and you've got WLEX."

"Thanks for the tip," the Man of Steel said as he rocketed away. "But when I get the Rabbit, it won't be to up your ratings."

Lex Luthor scowled after him. He could hardly believe the Man of Steel had turned down his offer of fame and riches. But if bribery didn't work, blackmail might. He had the feeling that he was about to learn a lot more about the Man of Steel.

"I planted a bug on him when I slapped him on the back, Happersen," Luthor said to the small, dark-haired man waiting in the shadows. "Don't lose him."

The Metrospire Hotel was a gleaming spiral reflecting the glitter of Metropolis at night. As the Man of Steel landed on the penthouse balcony, a voice purred from the room beyond, "Henry Johnson, or should I say, John Henry Irons! Come in, I was expecting you!"

The Man of Steel stepped into the light. "Angora!" he rumbled. "You? You're the White Rabbit? You're the one selling the Toastmasters on the streets?"

"And for old times' sake, I'm willing to share the profits," Angora, the woman known as the White

Rabbit, said. She was all white—her hair, skin, and clothing—stretched out on a white couch in an all-white living room.

Not long ago, the two of them had been colleagues, working for a U.S. government–sponsored weapons design firm. He was the resident ballistics genius. She was the computer-imaging whiz kid. They became friends, then, later, they fell in love. And then the guns he had designed for the army fell into Quraci hands. He had gone to the Middle Eastern nation of Qurac and seen the bodies of innocent women and children ripped apart by the very weapons he had invented. He blamed himself.

"I told you what I found in Qurac," John Henry Irons said, his eyes glittering angrily through the slits in his mask. "You knew why I destroyed the prototypes for my inventions, why I dropped out of sight and changed my name to Henry Johnson!"

Angora's laugh was like a growl. "But I was able to retrieve the designs. Now what do you say? It could be very profitable. You'd be rich and—"

The Man of Steel could hardly contain his fury. He reached for her, his metal gauntlet gleaming like the edge of a knife. "I'm not interested," he said through gritted teeth. "But maybe you'd like to tell that story to the cops."

He knows I sold the guns to Qurac, she thought.

He'll never join us. Swiftly, she reached beneath the sofa cushion, pulled out a customized Toastmaster pistol, and fired.

The impact sent the Man of Steel hurtling backward from the balcony. He fell fifty stories, then crashed into the fuel tank of an oil truck parked below. The truck exploded.

From high above, Superboy dived into the flames. The white-hot armor blistered his hands, but Superboy didn't drop the Man of Steel until he was well away from the fire.

"You okay?" Superboy asked.

"I'm fine, thanks to you!" said the Man of Steel. "My special armor helped protect me from the flames. What about you?" he asked as he struggled to his feet. "I thought as Superman's clone, you'd have his invulnerability!"

"Probably just psychosomatic blisters," the teenager assured him jokingly as he blew on his hands. But privately he, too, was surprised by the burns. He changed the subject. "Bet you're wondering what I'm doing here. I'd been following you, to apologize. And then I saw that woman shoot you," Superboy said. "I wanted to tell you that you were right. It's my fault that pilot died! Every time I think about it I want to kick myself!"

"I know how you feel," said the Man of Steel.

"But save it—we don't have the time now. Come on!"

The Man of Steel and Superboy flew into the air and up to the top of the Metrospire Hotel. They landed on the penthouse balcony and rushed inside—but the White Rabbit was gone.

"Who was she?" asked Superboy.

"Someone I knew a long time ago. I used to be a weapons designer," the Man of Steel growled. "She stole my design, and now she's selling the Toast-masters to gangs. That pilot was killed with a gun I invented. I'm afraid his death was as much my fault as it was yours!"

The bug planted on the Man of Steel was destroyed by the fire, but Happersen reported to Lex Luthor all he had learned. "John Henry Irons was a weapons designer who skipped out on his contract. He's wanted by the Feds!"

Excellent, thought Luthor. *I can control him through blackmail, even though he's already turned me down.* Then Luthor reconsidered. *But if he'd walk out on a federal project, he might not be malleable enough for my needs. No,* Luthor decided, *he isn't the one. Perhaps it's time I turned my attention to Superboy.*

Luthor's intercom buzzed, interrupting his

thoughts. "Mr. Luthor, Packard from Project Cadmus is here!" said Happersen.

"Send him in!" Luthor said. The pudgy little scientist stumbled into the room, wiping his damp palms against his trousers.

"Packard," Luthor said, "I pay you well for information on Cadmus. You told me they couldn't clone Superman."

"Well," said Packard nervously, "yes and no. Listen, Mr. Luthor, and I'll tell you everything."

As Luthor listened to Packard's explanation, he began to see how he might use this information to gain control of Superboy.

The blinding morning sun shone bright on the White House as a limousine drove sedately up to its iron fence. A senator carrying a briefcase stepped out and walked through the gate.

Suddenly, behind him, the limousine roared to life. It drove straight at the fence, ripping a hole through it as it careened onto the White House lawn. A van followed close behind, then screeched to a halt. Its doors flew open, and Quraci gunmen leapt out.

White House Security had the would-be assassins on camera. A guard punched a button, and the computerized automatic defense systems opened fire. Then, on the monitor screens of the security room, they saw a caped figure appear.

"It's Superman!" cried one of the security men. "He's fighting the assault squad."

"Which Superman?" someone asked, squinting into the screen.

Metal glinted off the left side of his face. "It's the Cyborg!"

"But the computers have orders to shoot any unidentified personnel within the perimeter!" another guard said. "That would mean him too!"

The Cyborg and the would-be assassins fought amid a rain of high-tech weaponry. One by one, the Cyborg felled the terrorists. A final Quraci struggled to his feet. With great effort, he raised a bazookalike cannon. "This shell's gonna level this whole block, and there's nothing you can do about it!" he sneered.

The Cyborg whirled. His mechanical hand flipped back, and a barrel emerged. He fried this last assassin with a searing blast. The terrorists had been defeated, but the automatic defense systems continued to fire at the Cyborg, as though he were the enemy.

Inside the White House, one of the technicians tried to override the computers, but they kept on firing. "Everything's on automatic now!" he exclaimed. "The computers don't recognize the Cyborg! There's nothing we can do to stop their fire."

"Oh, yes there is," said a young scientist. "If this guy is Superman like he says he is, then a retina scanner should identify him and coincide with the records on file." The scientist snatched up a hand-held scanner, ran into a room overlooking the White House lawn, and threw open a window.

Shouting instructions to the Cyborg, the scientist hurled the scanner high into the air. The Cyborg pushed off and caught the scanner. Protecting it from laser fire with his own body, he then held the scanner up to his humanoid eye.

Inside the security room, the computers flashed:

RETINA SCAN COMPLETE. DNA SCAN COMPLETE. PROCESSING. IDENTITY CONFIRMED.

The weapons stopped firing. A cheer rang out in the security room. The Cyborg, it seemed, was Superman. And he'd saved them all. With the young scientist beside him, the Cyborg marched into the White House security room.

"There is more here than meets the eye," the Cyborg said. "The attack may not be over. I need your intelligence information." Before their amazed eyes, the Cyborg's mechanical arm shifted, wires snaked out, and he linked himself directly into the massive security computer. Within moments, strategic and nonstrategic data on the United States, its allies, and its enemies encoded on his computerized mind, and the assassins were identified.

The Cyborg turned to the senator, who was still holding his briefcase. "The assassins stole plastique to build that bomb from a base in Europe," he explained. "This very briefcase had been purchased in London by one of the attackers. Your driver was a Quraci terrorist, substituted for your usual driver. He planted a bomb in a briefcase identical to yours, then switched cases. The one you hold contains that bomb. I suggest that you place it on the floor and move far back."

The Cyborg's mechanical eye glowed. Instantly, the briefcase melted, destroying the bomb.

A presidential aide rushed up. "The President wants to see you," he said.

As he stepped toward the President, the Cyborg's arm extruded a small component. "Take this," the Cyborg said as he handed the device to the President. "Use it to communicate with me whenever necessary."

Minutes later, the Cyborg left the White House and soared into the air. The President, his aides, the senator, and the scientists all looked after him, awestruck.

"It's really him," said the President. "He looks different, but Superman is really back!"

Eleven

Superboy landed behind a convertible that had skidded and was teetering precariously off the edge of the Hobsneck Bridge. He lifted the car high into the air. "Only the real Superman could do this!" he said, grinning triumphantly at the TV cameras.

"And only the real Supergirl could do *this*!" said a voice below him.

He looked down. Supergirl had flown beneath the section of the steel walkway that Superboy stood on and had lifted it, with one hand, into the air. "Lex Luthor would like you to join us for dinner, Superman," she said with a smile. "Around seven? At the LexCorp penthouse?"

Superboy gazed down at her. She was the most beautiful girl he had ever seen. "Uh . . . sure," he said. "I'll be there."

. . .

In a dingy apartment crammed with stolen merchandise, a short, plump little con man stood before a figure covered from head to toe in burgundy and gold skintight spandex. Pointed spikes loaded into small cannons were mounted on the man's wrists.

"The money will be in your Swiss bank account by midnight, Stinger. You got Rex Leech's word on that!" said the con man. "Just do what you were hired to do!"

As the Stinger sprang from the window, Leech reached for the phone. "It's done!" he said into the receiver. "Just remember—the kid's all mine!"

Superboy looked around Luthor's penthouse, impressed by its luxury.

"Glad you could join us, mate," Luthor said heartily.

Then Supergirl stepped into the room, wearing a low-cut pink evening dress. For the rest of the evening, Superboy had eyes only for her.

As they sat down to dinner, Luthor asked Superboy to come and work for WLEX, but Superboy refused. "WGBS treats me good!" he said.

"But LexCorp covers the world," said Supergirl. "Think how that could help. Plus, we could work together every day! Wouldn't that be fun?"

Superboy gazed at her admiringly. "What can I

say? I love a girl in uniform. 'Course, I love her out of uniform too. You want me . . . you got me!"

Hook, line, and sinker, thought Lex Luthor. "I'll have the contracts drawn up first thing tomorrow," he said.

Later that evening, inside a modern apartment building at 344 Clinton Street, Vinnie Edge, head of WGBS, spoke to Superboy. "When I read Clark Kent was one of the many who was killed by that Doomsday creature, my first thought was that his apartment was available . . . and that I knew a guy who needed an apartment." As Tana Moon looked on, Vinnie Edge handed Superboy the key. "Our close working relationship could possibly be misconstrued as a small conflict of interest, so I think a third party should manage your affairs," Vinnie continued. "This is my close personal friend, Mr. Rex Leech."

The little con man pumped Superboy's hand. "Mr. Edge found you these great digs. But I'm gonna make you rich!" he chortled.

Superboy was starting to tell them about his agreement with Lex Luthor when Rex Leech's daughter, Roxy, rushed into the room and threw herself into Superboy's arms. Gazing at him admiringly, the little blond ran her fingers through his hair. Superboy's eyes glazed over. "Okay," he sighed. "Where do I sign?"

"Great!" chortled Leech. "First we get you trade-marked, then we issue cease and desist orders on those other Superphonies!"

While Superboy signed the contract hiring Rex Leech as his business manager, Vinnie Edge turned to Tana. "Take an extra chopper and a second camera crew with you tomorrow," he said. "I think it'll be a big news day."

Tana was suspicious. "You've arranged for someone to attack Superboy, haven't you?" she said. "That's going too far!"

"The kid brings in the ratings," Vinnie growled. "Do what I say or you'll be replaced."

The next day, Superboy flew through Metropolis carrying a 1940s train locomotive toward the Museum of Science. Behind him flew Tana Moon and another WGBS chopper.

Suddenly, a rocket barrage knocked him off balance. The locomotive fell from his shoulders. Pedestrians scattered as it plummeted toward the ground.

Like a blur, Superboy rocketed toward the engine. He hit it with all his might, knocking it into a deserted park. It landed, nose down, half buried in the ground.

Superboy fumed. "Who attacked me?" Down an alley, he spotted a menacing figure.

Faster than a speeding bullet, Superboy flew

toward the villain—and ran into a rope strung across the alley. He flipped forward, crashed into a brick wall, and landed flat on his back.

The Stinger dived at him, but Superboy struggled to his feet and threw a vicious punch. The battle raged to the waterfront, near the footings to the Metropolis Bridge.

Out of nowhere, Supergirl appeared behind the Stinger. "Invisibility is another of my powers," she said with a smile. "It's a good thing Lex sent me to help his newest talent!"

Swiftly, the Stinger flipped out of her way—slamming right into Superboy's fist. The fallen Stinger raised his arms.

"He's surrendering." Superboy grinned.

Then suddenly, the Stinger rapid-fired his explosive spikes into the bridge's footings.

"You missed us!" said Superboy.

"Those are explosive charges, you moron!" the Stinger laughed as he leapt for safety.

Suddenly a shattering explosion shook the city. Half the Hobsneck Bridge collapsed into the river. Support cables snapped like rubber bands, and cars tumbled into the water.

From the safety of her helicopter, Tana Moon watched, horrified. Superboy and Supergirl and countless others had just died for TV ratings.

But as Tana stared, Superboy and Supergirl climbed from the rubble. Together they plunged into the river, through the murky water, to the crashed cars piled on the bottom. Working together, they quickly saved the people who were trapped there.

Meanwhile, in the Fortress of Solitude, robot drones scurried down a corridor, past a Kryptonian Battle Suit, toward an egg-shaped device which glowed and crackled with energy.

"The Master's Regeneration Matrix is experiencing an overload," the head drone said. "We have already shut down all solar receptors. There must be a release."

Suddenly a seam formed in the egg. Inside, a sleeping figure dressed in black Kryptonian garb began to awaken. The robots helped him into a floating Kryptonian chair.

"I want to know what's going on," the figure said.

The chair floated through the corridors and halted before giant monitor screens that showed the four beings—the Last Son of Krypton, the Man of Steel, Superboy, and the Cyborg—who each claimed to be the real Superman.

"Something must be done about this," the black-garbed figure said. He rose from his chair and marched with determination from the chamber toward the Kryptonian Battle Suit, black, gleaming, and menacing. It waited like a giant robot in the corridor.

The police had arrived at the collapsed bridge. Superboy had done all he could to help save those hit by the explosion, and now he was eager to go after the Stinger.

"You're going to be a member of the LexCorp family," Supergirl said. "We have a global information network and vast resources. We can help track that creep."

Superboy felt embarrassed, but he told her he had signed a contract with WGBS.

Supergirl sighed. Lex was going to be very angry.

In a dank alley in Hob's Bay, a youthful gang member fired at the Man of Steel from the shadows. Suddenly the teenager was fried by a bolt of energy from above.

The Man of Steel frowned as the Last Son of Krypton descended. "You may look like Superman," the Man of Steel rumbled, "but Superman would never have done that."

The Kryptonian, gritting his teeth in rage, punched the Man of Steel into the street as he roared, "I am the true Superman, and I will suffer no pretenders!"

The Man of Steel swung his hammer, knocking the Kryptonian back. Onlookers gathered, cheering first one, then the other.

Suddenly a process server pushed his way through the crowd. Bravely he shoved cease and desist orders at the two Supermen.

Electricity leapt from the Kryptonian's hands, frying the papers. The Man of Steel tackled the Kryptonian before he could fry the process server, as well, and roared skyward.

The Kryptonian sneered. "You like to fly high and fast? All right. Let's see how high and fast you can go!"

Everything became a blur as the Kryptonian dragged the Man of Steel into the stratosphere. "Stop, you idiot!" he cried.

The Man of Steel wrenched free and tumbled down in a great suborbital arc. Using his boot jets, he slowed his reentry.

The Kryptonian tackled him again. Together they plummeted Earthward, slamming into the parking lot of a suburban shopping mall on the outskirts of Coast City, California.

News choppers circled the impact crater formed by their landing as, against all odds, the Supermen staggered to their feet and continued to fight.

"You want me to believe you're Superman, then

act like Superman!" the Man of Steel rumbled. "Superman wouldn't have tried to fry a process server who was just doing his job. He wouldn't have pulled me into space. He wouldn't have crashed us here!" The Man of Steel punctuated each sentence with a blow.

"Don't you know what I could do to you?" asked the Kryptonian. "With a wave of my hand, I could destroy you!"

"What're you gonna do?" the Man of Steel growled. "Fry every Superman, until you're the only one left? That would disgrace the shield you wear on your chest. I can't let you do that!" With a massive blow, he shattered the Kryptonian's visor.

Suddenly, the crater was surrounded with police cars, their sirens wailing and lights flashing.

These flashing lights—they blind me! the Kryptonian thought as he staggered to his feet. *But perhaps I have been blind in other ways as well! There must be more to Superman than power. Perhaps it requires compassion . . . and a human heart.* The Kryptonian rose into the air. "Go back to Metropolis, then, Man of Steel," he shouted. "That city will be in good hands. I can hear the people of Coast City cry out for my help! And Superman . . . the one and only Superman . . . must answer!"

. . .

Lex Luthor watched the confrontation between the two Supermen on television. Surrounded by reporters, the victorious Man of Steel gave an interview. *He looks battered and exhausted,* Luthor thought. *Perhaps I can turn that to my advantage.*

Luthor called Dr. Happersen into his office and ordered him to find a cargo pilot to offer the Man of Steel a ride back to Metropolis. If he was lucky, the Man of Steel would take the bait.

Luthor smiled to himself. Now it was time to implement part two of his plan.

In Hob's Bay near the docks, Luthor's private army invaded the White Rabbit's hideout. Her enforcers were felled by gas grenades, but the Rabbit welcomed the attack with interest. She wondered what Lex Luthor wanted with her.

Back in the LexCorp Building, the White Rabbit waited for Luthor alone in a darkened room. When he opened the door, she rose, languidly, and slunk toward him.

"You must want something. Word is, the Man of Steel turned down your job offer. You can't own a man like that!" she murmured.

"That's why I'm giving him to you on a silver platter," Lex sneered. The Man of Steel had indeed taken the bait and was heading toward Metropolis aboard a LexFreight plane.

I know the Man of Steel's secret, Luthor thought to himself. *He backed out of a government contract and is hiding out from a federal agency. He left a very lucrative job to protect innocent women and children from the consequences of his inventions. He's responsible . . . but not naive, like Supergirl. If he worked for me, he would begin to question my motives . . . and I cannot afford to be questioned. Eventually I will own a Superman, but it will not be the Man of Steel. All of Metropolis knows about his war against gang violence, and it is best for all concerned that he die at the White Rabbit's hands.*

It was almost dawn when the LexFreight cargo jet landed at a small private airport on the outskirts of Metropolis. Led by the White Rabbit, a small army carrying Toastmasters was waiting in the shadows.

As the Man of Steel opened the cargo door, he was taken by surprise as a blast hit him squarely in the chest, blowing him out the back of the plane. He grabbed part of the torn fuselage and used it as a shield as he rocketed, through a hail of bullets, toward the White Rabbit and her crew. By the time he reached them, the shield was nearly useless, but he was now on top of them.

He dispatched the Rabbit's henchmen until only she herself was left. Then he dragged her into the air.

"Take me to the factory where the Toastmasters are assembled," he rumbled.

Moments later, the Man of Steel glared around the old abandoned factory. "So this is where they're manufactured," he said.

"The old hydraulic stamping press that used to make car fenders now pounds out cannon housings," the White Rabbit said. She moved toward a panel filled with switches, talking to distract him.

"Going to be hard to smash this operation, isn't it? Even with that great big steel hammer of yours! If you don't believe me, look around. Here! Let me turn on the light."

But the switch she threw wasn't a light switch. Suddenly a giant hook on a cable swung at the Man of Steel, hitting him in the chest. He crashed into the hydraulic press, which closed on him like a vise.

"That should hold you!" she said. She reached behind the press and activated a bomb she had hidden there for just such an emergency. "This old factory proved to be very inefficient. I've decided to move my manufacturing operations elsewhere. Its destruction will hardly affect my business, but it will affect you," she said with a sinister smile.

"No!" he shouted. His muscles bulged as, with superhuman effort, he lifted the press and broke free. The old press began to topple.

The Rabbit turned and ran. As the press fell toward her, the factory exploded. Glowing like a comet, the Man of Steel rocketed from the blast.

Just outside the orbit of the moon, an immense ship of intricate design came out of hyperspace.

"Earth is below us, Captain. As yet, the humans are unaware of our presence here," an alien crewman spoke as he stared into a screen.

"Excellent!" said the captain. He gazed out the window at the planet in the distance. "Superman is no longer there to protect the Earth. We may well be the last living beings to view it in its unaltered state!"

Twelve

A communications satellite focused on an unidentified object approaching Earth from the vast-
ness of space. The moving image was transmitted, via
satellite dish, to monitor stations within the LexCorp
Building. Scientists at the lab gathered around the
monitors, voicing their dismay. Mr. Luthor must be
notified at once, they decided.

Luthor stared at the monitor screens. The object appeared to be a ship. It was huge and deadly-
looking. Suddenly, mechanized cannons swiveled
toward the satellite and fired. The transmission
stopped abruptly.

"Inform NASA and the government," said Luthor.
"At once! That ship is approaching fast!"

"White House Security to Superman!"
Hovering over Metropolis, the Cyborg answered

the call, speaking to a presidential aide through the communication link he had given the President. "An alien ship is approaching Coast City in California," the aide said. The aide noted that the Last Son of Krypton was nearby, fighting a forest fire.

"If this is an attack, then the Kryptonian may be behind it," the Cyborg suggested. Then he clicked off the comlink and flew at superspeed for Coast City.

The citizens of Coast City gaped as a giant craft filled the sky, their amazement changing to horror as glowing "Carnage Globes" flew from the hatches of the ship.

From a distant suburb, the Last Son of Krypton rose up through the smoky haze of the forest fire and soared toward the ship. But the Cyborg swooped before him, blocking his way. "Move aside," the Last Son of Krypton shouted. "That ship could be a threat!"

The Cyborg blasted the Kryptonian back. "Our government thinks that *you* are the threat!" the Cyborg lied. "You are to be blamed for the deaths of millions!"

The Carnage Globes began to detonate. Shards of energy spiraled out, destroying neighborhoods, then shattering the city in an all-encompassing blast. Shock waves blasted both Supermen. The Last Son of Krypton fell, burned and in agony.

The ship hovered over the huge crater that had once been Coast City. *If my blast didn't kill the Kryptonian, the shock wave must have,* thought the Cyborg, satisfied.

Just then, smaller pods dropped from the ship and burrowed into the ground. Beneath the earth, they linked mechanically with other pods. Together they formed a vast Engine which was growing rapidly within the crater.

Surrounded by flame and desolation, the Last Son of Krypton staggered to his feet. "The Fortress of Solitude," he mumbled, realizing that there was a single chance for his survival. "Must get to Antarctica." With enormous effort he wobbled into the air and flew south.

Over the comlink, the President's aide sounded worried. NASA had tracked the ship, then lost it in the explosion. None of their satellites could pierce the smoke over Coast City. "Is the ship still there?" the aide asked.

"Coast City has been destroyed," the Cyborg reported back grimly. "A ring of fire surrounds it, billowing smoke into the air. The ship has vanished without a trace. So far I've found no one alive. But this is too big a job for me alone. Send Superboy. If he's really my clone, as he claims, then we'll work well together. Tell him I'll meet him on the other side of the Temblor mountain range." He then shut down the comlink.

Behind the hovering Cyborg, the ship descended to dock with the vast Engine, now a veritable Engine City. His metal parts glistening, the Cyborg landed on the ship's deck as the captain stepped from a hatch and knelt before him.

"You tricked them all, my lord," said the captain. "Many humans believe you are the real Superman. And even those who are unsure of your identity feel that you are a great hero. No one guesses your real purpose here is to abscond with their Earth."

"You played your part well also, Mongul," said the Cyborg, genially slapping the captain on the shoulder. "You perfectly timed your ship's release of the Engine Bomb and reshaped Coast City."

"Thank you, lord," said Captain Mongul, rising to his feet. "The first step went well, indeed. And, as we both know, Coast City will not be Earth's last Engine City!"

Meanwhile, a figure in a Kryptonian Battle Suit stalked across the Antarctic wasteland, toward the edge of a glacier. Dropping hundreds of feet into black water, the figure hit the steeply slanted side of the continental shelf and rolled until it hit the bottom.

Then it climbed to its feet and began to move along the ocean floor, an unstoppable juggernaut on a mission north.

Lois Lane and Jimmy Olsen huddled around a portable TV in the *Daily Planet* Building. The Cyborg, now joined by Superboy, announced they were going to apprehend the Kryptonian amid the desolation that surrounded Coast City. Against the Cyborg's advice, however, a WGBS news crew and military personnel would fly with them. Superboy dismissed the Cyborg's concerns with a wave. "With two of us looking after things? No sweat!"

The Cyborg sighed. "I was just as sure of my prowess and my own powers when I was your age."

Lois scowled at the screen. The Superman she knew hadn't had powers when he was Superboy's age, she thought to herself. Something wasn't right. If only she could put her finger on what it was.

The Cyborg, Superboy, and several military choppers filled with soldiers and reporters wearing respirators to filter the burning air flew over the Temblor mountain range toward Coast City.

Once hidden by the smoke pouring from the ring of fire, the Cyborg blasted away with his heat vision. The choppers exploded in flames.

Superboy dived to save their occupants, but the Cyborg blasted him to the ground. To cover his tracks, the Cyborg hurriedly told the presidential aide over the comlink that they had been ambushed. He was turning off the link in case the Kryptonian was using it to home in on them.

Then the Cyborg tackled Superboy. Superboy panicked. Grabbing the Cyborg's robot arm, he forced it back, and the mechanical arm flew apart.

"How did you do that?" the Cyborg growled.

"That's *my* secret," Superboy smirked. But he had no idea how he had done it either. He only wished he had.

"I can repair my hand later," the Cyborg sneered. "I don't need it to finish you off!" With his other hand he slammed Superboy into the base of Engine City.

Superboy didn't know how long he had been unconscious. He tried to lift his hand to hold his pounding head, but to his shock, he couldn't move his arm. His eyes flew open, and he looked around in alarm. He was bound, hand and foot, within a coffinlike machine. Only his head was free. *Where am I?* he wondered. *Why am I here?*

The ship's captain, Mongul, glared at the teenager. Mongul had fought and been defeated by Superman long ago. He had no love for anyone wearing the S-shield. *The Cyborg can defeat the others,* Mongul thought, *but one day, I will rule the Earth—alone.*

He activated a view screen, showing Superboy Engine City. "You're our prisoner here, boy," Mongul sneered. "For you there's no way out!"

Meanwhile, the Last Son of Krypton landed weakly on the Antarctic ice. With his remaining strength, he broke through to the Fortress of Solitude and staggered inside. Robot drones carried him to the Energy Matrix.

"No," the Kryptonian cried. "The Matrix is empty!"

"Superman, what is wrong?" the drone asked.

"I am not Superman. I am the Kryptonian artifact called the Eradicator. I built this Fortress. And now that the true Superman has returned, I must not fail him," the Eradicator gasped. Then he collapsed in a heap on the icy floor.

Obediently, the robots lifted him gently and placed him inside the Energy Matrix.

In the Media Room of Engine City, Mongul watched as the Cyborg interfaced with an editing machine that manipulated video images. He created a broadcast of himself and Superboy working together.

"The humans will believe that broadcast," the Cyborg said to Mongul, "as they have all the others." As the Cyborg began to describe what would happen next, Mongul leaned against a panel and secretly depressed a button. *Superboy has the right to know what is going to happen to his world,* Mongul thought, amused, *even if there's nothing he can do to stop it.*

In Superboy's prison cell, a monitor screen winked on. On it, the Cyborg was talking to Mongul. Superboy listened in growing horror to what the Cyborg had planned: Metropolis was going to be the next Engine City!

Superboy struggled desperately against his bonds. "I've got to get free! Metropolis . . . the whole world . . . is in danger," he said in panic.

Suddenly the machine that bound him flew apart and scattered over the floor. Superboy staggered to his feet, surprised. Even Superman couldn't have done that!

Avoiding patrols, he sneaked into the ship's ventilation system. *There isn't a chance I can beat the Cyborg alone,* he thought. *I've got to warn Metropolis! The Man of Steel will help me!*

After what seemed like hours, Superboy kicked out a vent and soared into the burning air. He wished he could fly faster, but he still felt weak. He'd be lucky to reach Metropolis by morning.

. . .

It was near dawn when alarmed LexCorp scientists showed Lex Luthor satellite images of a streak in the Atlantic Ocean, starting at the Antarctic and heading north.

"Whatever is making that streak is advancing rapidly enough to make a wake," said one of the scientists. "It appears to be heading for Metropolis."

"Get in touch with the LexScience research sub," said Luthor. "Tell them to find out what it is. When they do, put the sub commander through to me."

In his darkened workshop, the Man of Steel stared at a television as he removed his armor. The Cyborg was making another speech, saying that the visored Last Son of Krypton had destroyed Coast City. The Man of Steel couldn't believe it. *The Kryptonian virtually handed me Metropolis to protect,* he thought to himself. *But what if he just wanted me out of the way while he destroyed the city? I'm going to Coast City,* he decided. *I've got to help save the world—while there's still a world to save.*

Early that morning, Lois Lane walked into Perry White's office at the *Daily Planet*. "I don't trust the Cyborg," she said. "I'm going to find out what's really going on in Coast City."

Behind his desk, Perry White jumped to his feet. "Absolutely not!" he roared. "Walking into possible danger in pursuit of a story is one thing. Walking into a death trap is another."

Lois stormed out of his office. "I'm going to Coast City," she said. "There's nothing you can do to stop me!"

In the LexCorp Building, Supergirl stood before Lex Luthor. "The Cyborg thinks he and Superboy can handle whatever's happening in Coast City, but no one knows what that is," she said. "With all the smoke and debris it's impossible to see. And—"

Lex grabbed her arm, trying to shake some sense into her. "You're not going there. It's too danger-ous."

Supergirl looked at him accusingly. "That's what you said when Doomsday fought Superman. I didn't help until it was too late, and now Superman is dead. I'm going. I just wanted you to know where I was."

As she stepped toward the window, the phone rang. Luthor picked up the receiver, deliberately play-ing up the drama to keep her there.

"What?!" he shouted. "A giant robot? Heading for Metropolis?"

Supergirl eyed him, curious now but wary. "If this is a trick to keep me here, it won't work!"

Luthor clicked on the speaker phone. "It's no trick. Listen to the scientists who are observing it!"

The armored Kryptonian Battle Suit strode along the ocean bottom beneath the looming continental shelf, as a small, futuristic research sub floated nearby.

The robotlike figure seemed oblivious to them, the captain reported. Or maybe it didn't care. Maybe, like Doomsday, it knew there was nothing the humans could do to stop it!

"Drop a depth charge in the thing's path," said Luthor. "See how it reacts."

The charge exploded at its feet, but the robot didn't stop, the scientists reported. The rest of the report was lost in a rumbling sound, followed by screams and a deadly silence.

"What happened?" asked Supergirl.

An avalanche, thought Luthor, *caused by the shock waves from the explosion.* "I was afraid that might happen. The robot destroyed them," he lied. "You can't save them. But you can save Metropolis. At the speed it's traveling, that robot will be here in less than an hour."

Supergirl looked at Luthor steadily. *He's right,* she thought. *I can't leave Metropolis undefended.*

From her expression, Luthor knew what she was

thinking. "Go on, love," he said. "I'll meet you at the airport in half an hour."

Supergirl nodded. She moved to the window, which opened automatically, and leapt into the morning air.

Lois Lane was climbing into a small private jet when Supergirl flew overhead. The Man of Steel soared after her, then stopped and hovered. He looked surprised. Lois wondered what was going on. This was a lot of super-hero activity for a small private airfield. Lois started to run across the runway.

Across the airport, Supergirl landed beside the bay. Suddenly the Battle Suit, dark, glistening, and twelve feet tall, lurched from the water and onto the tarmac. Supergirl was waiting. With a massive psychokinetic punch, she smashed it to the ground.

Superboy weaved from side to side as he flew over Metropolis. Now that he was here, how could he find the Man of Steel? He was so tired he couldn't think straight. Then he heard a crash over by the airport. Hoping trouble hadn't started here already, he flew toward the bay.

As Supergirl fought the Battle Suit, Luthor circled overhead in his chopper.

The Man of Steel rocketed onto the scene. *What is he doing here?* Luthor wondered. *But maybe that robot will destroy him. Maybe they will destroy each other.*

"What's going on?" the Man of Steel shouted. "What is that thing?"

"It's a giant robot," Supergirl shouted. "It crushed a submarine and killed some scientists, and now it's attacking Metropolis!"

The Man of Steel fired a barrage of rivets at the Battle Suit, then rocketed into it. The Battle Suit toppled backward onto the tarmac.

Supergirl was ready to blast it again when Lois ran up and grabbed her arm. "Wait!" she cried. "If I didn't know better . . ." She took a deep breath and started again. "Superman once told me about a kind of Kryptonian armor he had as a memento. The way he described it, it would probably look a lot like that thing!"

Superboy landed beside the Man of Steel, gaping at the Battle Suit. "Are you saying that robot's got something to do with the real Superman, Miss Lane?" he asked, looking around at the others. " 'Cause otherwise, we're in trouble. Listen—Supergirl, Man of Steel—it's a long story, but the Cyborg is really the bad guy. There's a giant engine growing where Coast City used to be. And Metropolis is his next target!"

As Superboy spoke, a hatch in the body of the Battle Suit slid open and a man emerged.

It was Superman, dressed in a black costume, with a glowing S-shield on his chest, his hair long and shaggy. He dropped onto the runway with grim determination.

"Over my dead body!" he said.

Thirteen

News choppers and Team Luthor soldiers circled overhead as Superboy and the Man of Steel stepped protectively in front of Lois. The Man of Steel grabbed Superman's arm, causing him to wince. "If you're Superman, why aren't you invulnerable?" the Man of Steel demanded.

"I've had a lot to recover from," said Superman. "I was taken about as far down as anyone can go. That's why I needed that Kryptonian Battle Suit to get here." He turned to Lois. "Will you give me five minutes in private?"

Lois had waited for what seemed a lifetime for this moment. But now, as she stood before him inside a LexAir hangar, she couldn't let herself believe it was really him. Not without proof. The others had been convincing too.

"Did the others remind you of how I gave you

Ma's ring for our engagement?" Superman began. "Or about the time I told you I was really Clark? Or about that rainy day in July when we—"

Lois looked at him. Tears were running down her cheeks. She could hardly believe he'd come back. "But you were dead!" she said. "How can you be alive?"

Superman took her in his arms. "I . . . don't know," he said. "I woke up in my Fortress. I was very weak. I still don't have my powers. But there's a job to be done. Coast City is gone and Metropolis is threatened. Someone will pay. Just remember, no matter what happens, I will always love you."

He kissed her, then strode from the hangar.

Superman borrowed a pair of jet boots from one of the members of Team Luthor. "There's a man out there wearing my shield who has just killed millions of people," he said grimly as he strapped it on. "I'm going to make sure he's stopped." He rocketed into the sky. Superboy and the Man of Steel raced after him.

It might take years for the sun to recharge my solar-powered cells and renew my strength, Superman thought, *but powers or not, I will stop the mad Cyborg who has destroyed Coast City.*

On the deck of the mother ship, Mongul and the Cyborg stood overlooking Engine City.

"The warhead will soon be loaded with the armament needed to destroy Metropolis," said the Cyborg.

"Countless planets will cower before my military might!" roared Mongul. "And the fists of Mongul shall rule!"

The Cyborg blasted Mongul back. "*I* rule here. I tolerate your presence because I need soldiers. But if you displease me, I will bury you!"

Mongul picked himself up off the ground and glared at the Cyborg. *Don't be too sure,* he thought to himself. *I just might bury you!*

Superman, the Man of Steel, and Superboy descended through a smoky haze and dived, like avenging angels, toward Engine City.

From behind his mask, the Man of Steel studied Superman. He was beginning to think the guy might be the real thing, after all. "You know, Superman, going in there, you could die again."

"We could all die," Superman said grimly. "But I would gladly die to save Metropolis from the desolation that's below us."

The Man of Steel smashed through Engine City's outer wall. The others zoomed behind him through the hole and into the main gunnery room. Alien robots and soldiers attacked them, and they fired back. Despite the efforts of the others to protect him, a blast hit Superman in the legs, destroying his jet boots. Luckily, Superboy and the Man of Steel were able to drive the gunners from the room.

"We have to move before our friends come back with reinforcements," Superman said. He picked up a ray rifle from the floor and slung it over his shoulder. He looked at the others with a knowing grin as he reached for another. "I know the odds we're up against, and I'm not stupid. Some people say I'm the world's biggest Boy Scout. Well, you know the Scouts' motto—'Be prepared!' By the time he finished his speech he was wearing a dozen guns and ammo belts.

The three Supermen moved into a corridor. Before them was a staircase. "First we go down and make sure this place is totally inoperable," said Superman. "Then we head up and deal with Mongul and the Cyborg!"

Exchanging fire with alien attackers, they climbed half a mile down a spiral staircase until they reached the silo housing where the Engine Bomb was poised for its attack on Metropolis.

From one side of a high catwalk, an alien horde opened fire. The Man of Steel took the rear. Rays bounced off his back as the heroes scrambled out of range and rushed farther down the stairs. Below was the missile monitoring room. Suddenly a group of aliens surged up the stairs toward them.

Far below, the Engine Bomb roared to life, then slowly started to rise in the silo. A huge, deadly ring of fire from the missile's thrusters rushed up the silo's walls toward the Supermen.

"We're toast," groaned Superboy.

The Man of Steel grabbed Superman and threw himself against the monitor room door. It snapped open. "In here!" he shouted over his shoulder to Superboy.

Behind them, the alien horde was caught in the thruster's fire and incinerated.

The Man of Steel held the door shut as the Engine Bomb rocketed past. Then he looked around the control room. "Where's the kid? He was right behind me. He couldn't handle that fire!" He threw open the door. "Oh, Lord, don't let me have shut him out! Don't let me have caused his death!"

The catwalk was littered with charred corpses. It was impossible to tell if any of them was Superboy.

"Look!" called Superman from the monitor room.

On a view screen, Superboy was riding the Engine Bomb into the air over Engine City.

Between the G-forces and the wind, it was all Superboy could do to hang on to the Engine Bomb, yet he dug handholds in the metal casing as he slowly pulled himself up the missile toward the warhead. Finally, he was able to touch the bottommost row of Carnage Balls.

He closed his eyes, summoning his willpower, trying to turn on his disassembling power. He'd never done this before on demand, but now he had to. A city, maybe a world, depended on it!

The sphere Superboy touched exploded! He had done it, but it wasn't easy. He reached for another. Then he looked at the thousands of Carnage Balls covering the warhead.

I'll never destroy all of them in time, he thought. *I need a new plan!*

In the monitor room, Superman turned from the screen. "It's up to Superboy to save Metropolis. Our job is to make sure another Engine City is never launched."

Superman and the Man of Steel stepped from the monitor room over the charred bodies. The staircase spiraled down as far as they could see. "We'd better hurry," said Superman, as he stepped off the staircase into the abyss.

"Are you crazy?" The Man of Steel dived after him. "You don't have any powers!"

A half mile later, the Man of Steel shot past him

as Superman inexplicably slowed, then landed softly on the ground.

"I thought you couldn't fly anymore," the Man of Steel said, angry with Superman for scaring him half to death with that stunt.

Superman started to answer when a blast door irised open and an army of armored robots charged at them. Rays bounced off the Man of Steel's protective armor as he cleared a path with his hammer. Superman wielded his captured weapons, then winced as a heat ray slammed into the wall next to him.

Suddenly, the alien who had fired the heat ray flew backward, slamming into his partners, as if hit by an invisible ray.

What caused that? the Man of Steel wondered, but before he could say anything, the alien attackers increased their onslaught.

The Man of Steel and Superman fought furiously. Under their assault, the Cyborg's forces broke and ran.

"I just hope the kid is making out as well," the Man of Steel rumbled.

Now plastered against the nose cone, Superboy rode the Engine Bomb as it roared toward Metropolis. He had ripped off various panels, popped open others, even tried to rip out the rocket's innards. But the bomb hadn't stopped. Even if by some miracle he managed to disarm the thing, its speed would carry it into Metropolis. He had only one chance left.

Superboy clung to the nose cone, straining with all his might. He wasn't strong enough to stop the missile, but maybe he could change its course. Superboy grimaced, trying to use his little-understood telekinetic ability to redirect the missile up and away.

Throughout Metropolis, panicked crowds surged through the streets trying to get to safety.

Lex Luthor roared into a phone, ordering his people to find Supergirl. His city was about to be destroyed!

From the windows of the *Daily Planet* Building, Lois Lane, Perry White, and Jimmy Olsen stared up at the fast-approaching glow that filled the sky.

On the roof of the WGBS Building, newscaster Tana Moon stared at the approaching missile, bravely reporting Metropolis's final hour. Through her tears, she could see the tiny figure of Superboy, holding on helplessly to the missile's nose cone.

Just then, a few hundred feet before impact, the missile arced away from Metropolis. The city was lit by a blinding flash as the Engine Bomb exploded over the ocean.

From the window of his office in the *Daily Plan-*

et Building, Perry White shielded his eyes. "He did it!"

Superboy changed the course of the missile, Lois Lane thought, elated. *He saved us all!*

On the roof of the WGBS Building, Tana Moon stared blankly toward the spot where the Engine Bomb had ignited only moments before. "He was my friend," she sobbed. "He was my only friend. And now he's gone."

But not far away, a shaken Superboy fell from the sky and plowed a deep trench in a harborside landfill.

Minutes later, a LexCorp helicopter landed nearby. Luthor leapt from the chopper, rushed to Superboy, and hauled him to his feet. "Where is Supergirl?" he demanded.

"I don't know . . . what you're talking about!" Superboy said groggily. He had to help the other Supermen, he thought. Shoving Luthor aside, he wobbled up into the air.

The Cyborg angrily paced the Master Control Room of Engine City. Monitor screens showed the explosion over Metropolis. The Man of Steel and Superman were decimating Engine City's forces. And Lois Lane was saying this newest Superman was the *real* Superman.

Mongul stood to one side as the Cyborg ranted. Mongul had allowed Superboy to know the Cyborg's plans, hoping to exploit Superboy for his own purposes. But he had never thought the boy would be able to use the information against him and stop the destruction of Metropolis.

"If that fifth interloper is really Superman, doesn't that give you the chance for even greater revenge?" Mongul asked nervously.

"You are right!" said the Cyborg as he left the chamber. He would wipe out these Supermen as he had destroyed the pretender in the visor, the Last Son of Krypton.

In the Fortress of Solitude, the Eradicator twitched in his life-support tube, delirious and raving. "This must not be allowed," he moaned. "I must have more power."

The fluid in the life-support tubes began to bubble as the Fortress channeled its energy reserves into the Eradicator. Monitor banks went dark. Drones toppled. Then, in a blinding burst of light, the life-support tube shattered. The Fortress shook, and on the surface, the ice heaved as if from a monstrous underground explosion. A plume of energy shot up like a flame.

The Eradicator arose like a phoenix within this plume. His arms were outstretched, and his red eyes crackled with energy. He shot into the sky, leaving a glowing trail as he headed north to Engine City.

Superman and the Man of Steel ran through the bowels of Engine City, dodging gunfire. A ray from a side corridor seared the wall between them. The Man of Steel gaped as the robot that fired it flipped on its side and began to fly apart.

Just then Supergirl faded into view, standing with one foot on the killer robot.

"You've been with us the whole time?" asked the Man of Steel, astounded.

"She's been my secret weapon," said Superman.

The Man of Steel grinned as he shook her hand. "So what's our next move?" he asked.

Supergirl grinned back. If anyone could thwart the Cyborg's evil plan, it was this team, and she was glad to be a part of it.

In the Master Control Room of Engine City, Mongul lounged in the thronelike command chair. He wondered if the real Superman was indeed in Engine City. If the Cyborg was wrong about Superman's death, he might be wrong about many other things, as well.

Mongul slammed a button, initiating start-up procedures for the Engine.

"B-but, sir," said his lieutenant, "without the other balancing engines, this planet will spin uncontrollably out of orbit! It will rip itself apart!"

"I know," said Mongul grimly as he rose from his throne. "I have had enough of all these Supermen and their world. Let Earth be destroyed . . . there are plenty of other worlds to conquer."

If Superman still lives, Mongul thought, *it will make this revenge even more ironic. Engine City's fuel material was obtained with extreme difficulty, but it was worth it—the fuel is composed of the remains of Superman's home planet of Krypton!* Mongul laughed. *What better way to cause the demise of Superman's beloved Earth!*

Fourteen

As Supergirl flew far ahead, searching for the most direct path to the Engine Room, the two Supermen raced down the trembling corridors of Engine City. Then, from the darkness, Mongul stepped into the corridor far ahead. Even at that distance, Superman recognized him immediately from a previous battle they had fought years before.

"Feel the ground shudder?" laughed Mongul. "I have fired the giant rocket that is Engine City. Its thrust will send your Earth spinning out of orbit. Your planet will shatter into a million pieces."

"Earth is doomed unless we stop the blast!" Superman muttered grimly to the Man of Steel. "You stop the rocket while I take on Mongul."

The Man of Steel ripped off his mask. He wanted Superman to see his face. "You saved my life once. I took the name 'Man of Steel,' your name, and tried to make this life you saved count for something. The name's John Henry Irons."

Superman shook his hand. "Irons. But tempered steel, all the same. Good luck!"

As John Henry rocketed overhead, Superman fired at Mongul, blowing him back.

"You have no powers, Superman!" Mongul chortled as he fought through the spray of gunfire. "I will destroy you. Only then will I deign to deal with your Man of Steel." He slammed Superman back hard into the wall.

From the airport, Lois Lane called Clark's parents on a pay phone. "I'm still trying to get to Coast City," she said. "They've closed down flights heading west, but I'm not giving up yet." She took a deep breath and closed her eyes. "I think Clark's really back this time! I believe that's him!"

At the Kent farm, Martha and Jonathan huddled with their heads together so they could both listen and talk on the phone. "I pray to God you're right," said Martha. "I just hope we don't lose him again."

The Man of Steel rocketed onto a catwalk in the middle of the vast Engine Room. The power plant that ran Engine City rose above and below him, and a globe glowing with an eerie green light loomed high overhead. Pipes ran from the globe to a gigantic engine, which rippled with moving pistons and gears. Other pipes connected the engine to a huge, donut-shaped vessel far below.

What have I gotten myself into? the Man of Steel wondered. *I don't even understand how that thing works. How can I stop it?*

In the computerized core of Engine City, the Cyborg reached out his robot arm. Wires sprang from it to interface with Engine City's computer banks. He could now see and hear through Engine City's sensors. He knew Mongul was fighting Superman. He knew the Man of Steel was in the Engine Room. He knew that another, invisible being was wandering the ship. And he realized that the sequence had begun which would fire the rocket and send the Earth spinning out of orbit.

Mongul must have lost faith in my ability to transform the Earth into a vast warship to travel the galaxies, the Cyborg thought. *He's trying to take matters into his own hands, but I cannot let that fool destroy all I've worked for. I will lead Superman's invisible ally to the fight to aid Superman in the defeat of Mongul while I disrupt the firing process. Only then will I be free to confront Superman myself.*

The Cyborg went into a trance state. Then, leaving

enough consciousness behind to maintain his body's basic function, he left it and traveled as a wave of pure energy through the computer system of the ship and into Engine City's Master Control Room. He tried to interrupt the Engine's firing sequence, but his access to that technology had been blocked by Mongul.

Then, still traveling as energy waves, he flowed into the Engine Room, where, using pipes, wires, and circuits in the wall, he created for himself a new robot body. The Cyborg, now all machine, dropped from the ceiling and landed on the catwalk before the Man of Steel.

"Impressive, isn't it?" croaked the Cyborg. "Engine City is powered by a process too complicated for mere humans to comprehend—as my own power to animate mechanical objects is also beyond your understanding."

"You're the Cyborg in a new form, right?" the Man of Steel asked as he slammed him back with his hammer. *The process that powers Engine City is complicated,* he thought. *I need to keep that monster talking until I learn how to stop the Engine.*

"You've got a big rocket engine here . . . but it isn't going to work!" the Man of Steel said aloud, as he dodged the Cyborg's fire.

"Kryptonite fission will jump-start the fusion reactor via the engine before you. It creates the magnetic fields within the reactor that encourage and contain the fusion process. Why shouldn't it work?" the Cyborg said, lunging menacingly.

The Man of Steel knew he couldn't stop the fission process, but he might be able to interrupt the transfer of energy by destroying the Engine. With all of his strength, he swung his hammer at the Cyborg. With a *klang!* the metal head spun from the body and dropped among the gears of the Engine that whirled below.

The Man of Steel tackled the metal body. *I'll die in the attempt, but I'll beat this thing,* he thought. He dived among the cogs and pistons. *Like grit in the gears, I'll grind this Engine to a halt.* The thought was lost as pounding pain exploded through his body. He was being crushed, but he could feel the machine lurch and start to make a grinding sound.

A large gear popped out of sequence and ground against another. Pistons misfired. *I've done it!* the Man of Steel thought. *I've done it!* Then, with a roar like the end of the world, the Engine exploded, belching smoke and flame.

Many levels above, the lurching ship threw Superman to his knees. *John Henry must have succeeded,* he thought with a sigh of relief.

Seeing Superman off balance, Mongul kicked out at him—and connected hard with thin air. Suddenly Mongul was hurled back by a psychokinetic blast.

Superman has an invisible secret weapon, thought Mongul, *but not invisible for long!* He wrenched an overhead pipe from its housing and sprayed the air with oil. It coated the corridor, as well as Superman and Supergirl. She shook her head, blinded by the viscous fluid.

Mongul knocked her unconscious and pounded Superman into the floor. Engine City shuddered and became still. Then the lights began to dim.

"The Engine!" Mongul cried. "The Man of Steel has stopped the Engine!" He turned down the corridor and ran in a panic for his ship.

Even as the Cyborg's metal body was crushed between the Engine's gears, his Life-Energy leapt from the twisted metal and traveled back through the ship. Finally it returned to his Cyborg body, which was still plugged into Engine City's computer system.

The Earth has been saved, the Cyborg thought as he monitored the condition of Engine City. *This structure is running on emergency power. Mongul may have defeated Superman but I will deal with the traitor Mongul, for I need him no longer.*

. . .

Mongul raced into his ship and slammed the hatch. "We've got to get away! Now!" he shouted to the technicians manning the bridge. "Blast off!"

The ship undocked from Engine City and roared toward space. But unknown to Mongul, the Cyborg had sent his Life-Energy to possess the ship. As the ship rose into space, its self-destruct sequence began.

The ship exploded, billowing smoke and flame. Then, trailing fire, it plunged into the Pacific.

The Cyborg's Life-Energy returned to Engine City. He was satisfied. He had punished one enemy. Now it was Superman's turn.

Engine City continued to belch smoke and flame as the Eradicator hovered above it. Superboy flew up beside him. "We thought you were dead," Superboy said. "The real Superman is inside. I guess he wasn't dead either."

"He was dead," said the Eradicator.

Whatever he meant by that, it would have to wait, thought Superboy. He supposed he'd find out eventually. But right now, they'd better hurry. "Come on," Superboy said. "I can get us inside."

Inside the Engine Room, a final gear tumbled down from the shuddering engine. The Man of Steel fell from the machine and rolled to his side. His armor was shredded, and he was cut and bleeding. But he was alive.

My suit's tough, he thought as he struggled to his feet. *But it wasn't tough enough to save me alone. The metal robot body I tackled wedged in the Engine and helped protect me.*

Putting one foot unsteadily in front of the other, he staggered toward the corridor where he had left Superman. *Has Superman survived the fight against Mongul?* the Man of Steel wondered. He had to know quickly, and in his condition, walking was much too slow.

Taking a chance, he ignited the thrusters in his boots and rose unsteadily into the air. He was on his way, and one way or another, the Cyborg was going to be stopped.

Through a dimly lit corridor, Supergirl crawled toward the fallen Superman. He opened his eyes and, ignoring his pain, struggled to his feet. "We're lucky to be alive," he said. "Come on, we've got to stop the Cyborg." Together, gaining strength as they walked, they staggered down the corridor.

Minutes later, the Man of Steel landed beside them. "I may be a pile of crushed and shredded junk, but at least the jet boots still work. And I look a lot better than you do!" He grinned at Superman through swollen lips.

"Not by much," said Superman quietly. "You stopped the Engine?"

"It won't be in any shape to blast off for a very long time!" the Man of Steel answered.

Suddenly they heard a scream of maniacal laughter as the Cyborg zoomed overhead, this time in his own body. "I think he wants us to follow him," the Man of Steel said.

As they charged down the corridor, pipes and cables, controlled by the Cyborg, lashed out at the Man of Steel and Supergirl. Then the Cyborg realized he had a more interesting way to separate them from Superman. He took control of what was left of the Man of Steel's computerized armor.

The Man of Steel raised his arm and fired a round of rivets at Superman and Supergirl. "Run! Get out of the way! I can't stop myself!" he screamed.

Suddenly the armor's metal collar closed tightly around the Man of Steel's throat. "He can't breathe," said Superman. "Supergirl, help him, while I go after the Cyborg."

As Superman ran forward, Supergirl flew to help the Man of Steel, but his armor wouldn't budge. Suddenly Superboy landed beside her. "Here, let me do that!" he said. Supergirl was surprised to see him, but she moved back to give him room. He closed his eyes, concentrating as he used his telekinetic power. The rivets fastening the Man of Steel's collar flew into the air, releasing him from its grip. As the Man of Steel gulped in huge breaths, Superboy told them that the Last Son of Krypton, now revealed to be the Eradicator, was also in Engine City and was looking for Superman.

As Superman stalked toward the control room housing the Cyborg, the Eradicator landed beside him. He had left Superboy to aid the others, he said, and come to look for Superman alone.

"So *you're* the fourth new Superman!" said Superman. He had time to ask just one question, "Do you know why the Cyborg wants to destroy the Earth?"

Suddenly a metallic face formed in the wall. "I'm the Cyborg, Superman! And I can speak for myself!" he said. "My name is Hank Henshaw! You might remember me. I was once a human astronaut circling the Earth with three others. We were struck by cosmic rays that gave us powers, then killed us. But unknown to you, I didn't die. My power allowed my intelligence to journey as energy into my ship's computer. I was no longer human . . . and for all of your vast power, you could do nothing to aid me!"

"I do remember you," said Superman. "But why—?"

"I nursed my resentment as I formed a new body from twisted machinery," the Cyborg continued, ignoring Superman's question. "When I went to visit my beloved wife, I terrified her. She collapsed at the sight of me. And, powerful as you claimed to be, you could not save her!"

"I'm not God," Superman said. "I have no power over life and death!"

"You don't?" shouted the Cyborg. "Then how are you here?" In a calmer voice he continued, "In despair, I leapt into space, via a satellite transmission. For a while I possessed your Birth Matrix Chamber, which you had placed in orbit around the Earth. There I learned much about you, and devised a way to make you pay for everything. Then, forming a new body from a piece of your Matrix Chamber, I rocketed into space."

"You blamed me," said Superman. "But why did you choose to punish the Earth?"

"It was my Earth no longer, for I was no longer human," the Cyborg stated grimly. "I landed on a backward agricultural planet in the Andromeda system. The only technology there was Mongul's conquering flagship. I entered it and learned that you had once defeated him and that he too had a reason to hate you."

"And I suppose that flagship brought you here to Earth?" asked the Eradicator.

"Of course," the Cyborg answered. "When I began to improve on his ship's design, Mongul was alarmed—until I offered him revenge against the Earth and Superman. I assured Mongul that I could create a vast warship to travel the galaxies, not out of raw material, but out of Earth itself."

"All this to take revenge on me?" Superman asked.

"At first, but you had cheated me," said the Cyborg. "For as Mongul's ship approached Earth, I learned that you were dead. I knew then that I would make sure the Earth remembered you as a monster—a man who came back from death to destroy his adopted planet."

"I assume that this is where the Matrix comes into play again?" the Eradicator said.

"Very astute," the Cyborg assured him sneeringly. "Using the genetic codes and Kryptonian materials I stole from the Matrix, I fashioned myself a new body—half Kryptonian flesh, half Kryptonian metal—and called myself Superman. Then I raced ahead of Mongul's ship to Earth. The rest you know!"

As the mechanized Hank Henshaw faded back into the circuits and pipes, Superman shouted after him, "There was nothing I could do! Not for you.

Nor for your wife. I had no idea you blamed me . . . or hated me so!"

Suddenly, a door at the end of the corridor slid open noiselessly, beckoning them.

The Eradicator had listened to the Cyborg closely. "If the Cyborg's powers are from the Matrix Chamber, and he's part Kryptonian in nature, I might be able to successfully oppose him," he whispered.

Superman frowned. He and the Eradicator had clashed before. He seemed to have changed now, but . . . had he really?

Suddenly, pipes, hoses, and circuits ripped from the wall, pummeling the heroes and driving them toward the open door at the end of the corridor. The Eradicator leapt forward to protect the still-weakened Superman. *Perhaps he really has changed,* Superman thought.

As if reading his mind, the Eradicator said, "I also helped you when you were dead! I was programmed to protect the ultimate integrity of Kryptonian life. Your death awakened me," said the Eradicator, shattering a tangle of wires that slashed at them like a whip. "I was able to get to you quickly. Your body was not beyond repair, and your unique Kryptonian physiology still stored solar energy, which I combined with my own to bring you back."

Superman and the Eradicator fought against the

machinery stubbornly, but slowly, inexorably, they were being pushed toward the end of the corridor. They tumbled into a room lit by a glowing Kryptonite asteroid in a transparent chamber. Pipes led from the chamber into the room and beyond.

The Cyborg stood before it. "This asteroid is the ultimate power source of Engine City!" he said. "And the one fitting way for Superman to die . . . from exposure to a chunk of his home planet—Krypton!" The Cyborg slammed the container, cracking it with his metal fist. Deadly Kryptonite radiation began to leak into the room.

The Man of Steel, Superboy, and Supergirl rushed down the corridor toward the open door. They had seen Superman and the Eradicator enter the room and were hurrying to aid them.

Superman knew that if he allowed them to enter the room, not only he, but all of them, could die from exposure to the radioactive rock. He hit a control panel. The door closed, locking the others safely outside.

Weakened by the Kryptonite, Superman stumbled. The Cyborg lunged toward him, but the Eradicator stepped between them. Raising his hand, the Eradicator blasted the Cyborg back. The Cyborg screamed in pain.

Why is the Cyborg vulnerable to my power now, when he wasn't before? the Eradicator wondered.

Like Superman, he must be affected by the Kryptonite. It has made him susceptible to my power! And yet, somehow, I'm absorbing the Kryptonite energy.

Superman punched the Cyborg back. The Cyborg tried to reshape his body but no longer could. Nor could he control any of the other machines in the room. Screaming that he could easily sacrifice this body, the Cyborg grabbed one of the hoses coming from the Kryptonite asteroid, pointed it at Superman, and opened the valve. Kryptonite energy streamed from the hose straight at Superman.

"I gladly give my life to protect the last true Kryptonian," cried the Eradicator, leaping forward to shield Superman with his body.

The Eradicator screamed in agony as the lethal green-hued energy passed through him and emerged as a bright blue ray of light. The light struck Superman, surrounding him with a blinding aura. Then, suddenly, the Kryptonite asteroid atomized and turned to dust, its energy totally depleted.

With a thud, the door flew open. Superboy, the Man of Steel, and Supergirl rushed into the room. The Eradicator lay on the ground, burned and in agony. But Superman was glowing with power.

Superman whirled on the Cyborg. "You've disgraced the shield you wear!" he growled, then hit the Cyborg with all his now-massive strength.

The Cyborg blocked the blow, then tried to return it. But his powers had been diminished, while Superman's had fully returned.

The others watched, cheering, knowing that this battle was Superman's alone to fight. A final blow shattered the Cyborg's jaw into a thousand pieces, and his broken body fell and did not rise again.

The battle was over. Superman had won.

He reached for the cloak the Cyborg had worn and wrapped it around his shoulders. But the picture wasn't complete. Using her power to re-form matter, Supergirl altered the molecules of Superman's black Kryptonian bodysuit, changing it into his original blue and red costume.

"Awesome!" cheered Superboy. "*Now* you can call me Superboy . . . 'cause *that* dude is the only *Superman*!"

Superman left Superboy, Supergirl, and the Man of Steel to care for the Eradicator and monitor Engine City. Then he took off into the air. "I have urgent business in Metropolis," he said.

Lois Lane sat staring at the TV in her apartment, as she had all night long. Behind the fluttering curtains, the sky was brightening to dawn, but she didn't notice. She wished she had been able to get to Coast City. No danger could be as painful as waiting and not knowing.

Suddenly, there was a tapping at the window. *Probably just another bird,* she thought. But could it be? Her heart raced as she rushed over and threw back the curtains.

Outside, looking back at her, was Superman. The original. Alive. Clothed in his costume. His eyes shining with love.

"Clark!" she cried. Lois leapt joyfully from the open window, and was caught and held in Clark's strong arms.

Superman was back! And the Earth had been saved. He had died, and by a miracle, he had been reborn. *An experience like that could change a man. Will he be different now?* she wondered.

Lois hugged him close. "You know, we've got to bring Clark Kent back too," she murmured. "People will wonder."

Superman laughed joyously as he held her close. "Oh, he's back . . . but I think the rest of the world will find him in that forgotten fallout shelter under Baker Street. And something tells me that he's just as glad as I am to be alive!"

Superman had been victorious in the fight of his life. By a miracle, he had survived even death. The world had been saved. The people he loved most, Lois and Ma and Pa, were finally safe from harm. Holding

Lois tightly in his arms, Superman soared joyously into the sky over Metropolis.

"Look! Up in the sky!" a cop walking his beat called out.

"It's a bird!" A grocer opening his store shaded his eyes as he stared into the morning sky.

A woman walking her dog squinted up and corrected him. "No! It's a plane!"

"You're both wrong!" said a boy, a huge grin spreading over his face. "It's Superman!"

About the Author

Louise Simonson was born in Atlanta, Georgia, where she attended Georgia State University. She began her publishing career in New York City. Her first job in comics was at Warren Publishing, a small comic-book company, where she eventually became vice president and senior editor. In 1980 she began working for Marvel Comics, where she edited numerous titles, including *Star Wars* and *The Uncanny X-Men*. She left her editorial position to pursue her freelance writing career, creating the award-winning Power Pack series. Among other titles, she wrote *X-Factor*, *The New Mutants*, and *Web of Spider-Man*. Since coming to DC Comics, Simonson has scripted *Batman* and *The New Titans* and continues to write *Superman: The Man of Steel*, where she is closely involved with formulating continuity between the four Superman titles.

Ms. Simonson lives in upstate New York with her husband, Walter, who is also a comic book writer and artist.

About the Illustrators

José Luis García-López was born in Pontevedra, Spain, and raised in Buenos Aires, Argentina, where he began drawing on every blank piece of paper he could find. He moved to New York in the 1970s and has worked for Western Publishing, Charlton Comics, and DC Comics. García-López is an award-winning illustrator with a long and illustrious career pencilling and inking almost every character in the DC Universe, including Batman, Robin, the Teen Titans, Wonder Woman, the Flash, and Superman.

Dan Jurgens was born in 1959 in the Smallvillelike town of Ortonville, Minnesota, where he was exposed to the wonderful world of comics by way of his interest in the *Batman* television show. Shortly after that, Dan decided to seek a career in comics. After high school, he majored in graphic design at the Minneapolis College of Art and Design and, after graduating in 1981, went to work for DC Comics as an artist on *Warlord*. Over the years he became writer and artist of such titles as *Sun Devils, Booster Gold, Flash Gordon,* and *Superman* (including the record-breaking comic book, *Superman #75*, the historic issue where the Man of Steel died). Jurgens currently lives in Minnesota with his wife and two children, where he is hard at work on a number of exciting new projects.

Alex Ross is a graduate of the American Academy of Art in Chicago. Abandoning a promising career in advertising after three years (a period he refers to as "a living redundancy"), he is currently working on *Marvels*, a fully painted miniseries for Marvel Comics, due for release in the winter of 1993.